D1180586

Valiant

www.**rbooks**.co.uk
www.**bbc**.co.uk/**merlin**

Also available:

The Dragon's Call

Coming soon:

The Mark of Nimueh

The Poisoned Chalice

For younger readers:

The Magic Begins

Potions and Poison

Coming soon for younger readers:

A Fighting Chance

Sword and Sorcery

Valiant

Text by Mike Tucker

Based on the story by Howard Overman

BANTAM BOOKS

MERLIN: VALIANT
A BANTAM BOOK 978 0 553 82110 9

First published in Great Britain by Bantam,
an imprint of Random House Children's Books
A Random House Group Company

This edition published 2009

1 3 5 7 9 10 8 6 4 2

The Random House Group Limited supports the Forest Stewardship Council
(FSC), the leading international forest certification organization. All our titles that
are printed on Greenpeace-approved FSC-certified paper carry the FSC logo.
Our paper procurement policy can be found at www.rbooks.co.uk/environment.

Mixed Sources
Product group from well-managed
forests and other controlled sources
www.fsc.org Cert no. TT-COC-2139
© 1996 Forest Stewardship Council

Typeset in Bembo by Falcon Oast Graphic Art Ltd.

Bantam Books are published by Random House Children's Books,
61–63 Uxbridge Road, London W5 5SA

www.**kids**at**randomhouse**.co.uk
www.**rbooks**.co.uk

Addresses for companies within The Random House Group Limited can
be found at: www.randomhouse.co.uk/offices.htm

THE RANDOM HOUSE GROUP Limited Reg. No. 954009

A CIP catalogue record for this book is available from the British Library.

Printed in the UK by CPI Mackays, Chatham, ME5 8TD

With grateful thanks to Johnny Capps,
Julian Murphy, Polly Buckle, Rachel Knight,
Sarah Dollard, Jamie Munro, Pindy O'Brien,
Filiz Tosun, Anna Nettle and Rebecca Morris

Chapter One

The storm bore down mercilessly on the hillside town. Dark, swollen clouds raced across the sky like black wolves, obscuring the pale moon that struggled to rise in the sky and turning evening into night. Fat raindrops started to fall, slowly at first but with gathering momentum until the ground was sodden and slick.

Villagers hurried for houses which stood huddled beneath the shelter of the forest, as fingers of lightning danced and crackled above the treetops and thunder echoed around the valley below. Smoke from a dozen or more chimneys was snatched up by the wind and sent spiralling away like pale wraiths searching for victims.

Robert Mayer cursed under his breath as a gust of wind caught the awning over his stall, whipping it back and sending water cascading over the meagre display of vegetables that he had on show. Market day here was rapidly becoming a disaster as fewer and fewer people bothered to make the long trek up from the valley below. This storm would do nothing to help matters. He had only just sold enough to cover the feed for his horse. It had barely been worth the effort of setting up shop at all.

With a weary sigh of resignation he started to untie the rain-soaked awning. There was no chance that he would sell anything more today, perhaps next week would be better.

A noise made him turn. A figure on horseback emerged from the swirling tendrils of wood smoke, a dark cloak pulled tight around his head and shoulders. The horse's hooves clacked on the wet cobbles of the street. Villagers rushed past, heads bowed against the rain. Strangers rarely came to this place, and when they did no good ever came of it.

Robert Mayer watched as the horseman rode slowly down the main street. He stopped at a tangle of shabby wagons and hastily erected stalls that formed the market. Stallholders hurried to bring in goods from the driving rain and lash down awnings that flailed in the strengthening wind.

The horseman slid from his mount, securing the reins to a low post. He turned and looked at Mayer.

'You there,' he called. 'Where would I find Devlin?'

Mayer gave a snort of disgust. Devlin. Strangers, when they came, always came for Devlin. The village should have kicked out that shabby excuse for a sorcerer a long time ago. He spat into the mud and busied himself with his stall.

'Do I look as though I have time to give directions?'

'No,' said the stranger. 'You look like a fat, insolent peasant with no manners who needs to be taught a lesson.'

Mayer turned, his face flushing and anger rising in his chest. 'You will regret that.' He reached for the heavy mallet at his belt, striding through the mud towards the man who had insulted him.

There was a flash of steel and a sword blade sliced through the driving rain, coming to rest at Mayer's throat. The stallholder gasped in pain as the sword's tip pierced his skin.

The horseman pulled at the ties of his cape, letting it drop open. Mayer's eyes widened as he glimpsed the armour and colours of a knight of the realm.

'Forgive me,' stammered Mayer. 'I did not know . . .'

The knight smiled, but it wasn't a pleasant smile. It

was more of a sneer. A tall man with close-cropped hair and piercing grey eyes, he held himself like a warrior, tense, poised, always watching. He might have been described as handsome once, but the skin of his face bore the signs of too much time spent on the battlefield, and there was something about the set of his jaw, the curl of his lip, that gave his face a cruel edge and said that this was not a man to be trifled with.

He watched with amusement as a rivulet of blood trickled down the length of his glistening sword blade, then he turned to Mayer, fixing him with a piercing stare.

'Well, now you do know.' The knight twisted the tip of his sword and Mayer winced in pain.

'Please, Sir . . .'

'Valiant.'

'Sir Valiant. I meant no disrespect.'

'Really? Then I'll ask you again. Where will I find Devlin?'

Mayer pointed a trembling finger towards the far end of the market. 'His is the last stall, at the far end of the street.'

The knight removed his sword from Mayer's throat, wiping the blood from the blade with the edge of his sodden cloak. 'Tend to my horse, and be quick about it. I do not intend to be here long.'

'At once, sir.'

Mayer watched the knight stride purposefully through the tangle of stalls, villagers moving to get out of his way. He touched the wound at his throat. He had been stupid, and was lucky to escape with his life. It was always the same when strangers came to see Devlin – each time they brought trouble with them.

'We really should have kicked him out years ago,' he growled.

As Valiant made his way through the market, he smiled to himself – there was nothing quite like the livery of a knight to strike fear and awe into the hearts of peasants.

The stalls at the far end of the village were clustered more closely together than at the other end, their wares displayed less prominently. Dim firelight guttered in heavy torches. Valiant could see strange runic symbols, pentagrams and other mystical paraphernalia being hurriedly hidden from view as he passed.

Small wonder. These people were dicing with death by buying and selling occult items so openly. If Uther Pendragon knew of their trade . . . But then, if Uther Pendragon knew that a knight of the realm was here amongst them and what he intended to do . . . Valiant gave a snort of amusement. The king would never know.

He pushed aside a line of sodden blankets hanging across the street. Through the wood smoke and driving rain he could see the stall that the stallholder had described, a collection of rickety tables and hastily assembled shelves huddled within the crumbling stone walls of a disued building. Heavy canvas had been strung from the building's roof to try and give some shelter from the downpour. Valiant pushed aside the fabric with the tip of his sword and slipped inside.

The interior was dark and laced with the aroma of unfamiliar herbs and strange spices, but it was warm and dry, and despite the distaste he felt being in this environ-ment Valiant was grateful to be out of the storm.

He peered past the jumble of strange-shaped objects that hung from the tent poles and lay in untidy piles on tables. At the rear of the tent he could see a lone figure hunched over a flickering brazier.

Devlin.

The sorcerer looked up as Valiant stepped into the firelight, then he bowed his head.

'Sir Valiant.'

'I understand you have a shield for me.'

Devlin nodded and gestured towards a shrouded shape resting on a table near the fire. He crossed to the table and with a flourish flung back the cloth.

Valiant stared. The shield itself was nothing special, a gentle curve of burnished steel, the handle on its back held in place with leather straps, but the design that was painted upon its surface . . .

Three serpents coiled and writhed across the shield's face, every scale on their bodies painted in exquisite detail. The three mouths, gaping wide, revealed wickedly pointed fangs, their tips dripping with venom, while the eyes of the snakes glared malevolently. It was a shield designed to strike fear into the hearts of those who faced it.

Valiant reached out with a gloved hand but Devlin caught his wrist and gave a shake of his head. 'I wouldn't, sire. The serpents of the Forest of Balor have the deadliest of venom. With your swordcraft and this shield, I guarantee you victory.'

Valiant shook himself free of the sorcerer's grasp.

'Show me how it works.'

Devlin stretched out his hands towards the shield. He took a deep breath and started to mutter – deep, guttural, unfamiliar words. His eyes rolled backwards in his skull, their whites glinting in the firelight.

With a sudden hiss of anger the snakes erupted from the surface of the shield, their black, sinuous bodies bulging free from the metal, their tails still part of the metal surface, their heads bobbing and weaving as they searched for their prey.

Valiant took an involuntary step backwards, sword raised. These were like no snakes he had ever seen before. These were ancient, deadly things of myth.

Devlin watched with amusement as Valiant stared, transfixed by the writhing snakes.

'When you are competing in the tournament, you pin your opponent under the shield and then' – he stabbed two fingers towards Valiant's face – 'a snake strikes! Your opponent will be paralysed in seconds!'

Valiant nodded, still keeping his eyes on the snakes. The shield was better than he could have hoped for. A frown flickered across his brow.

'How do I bring the snakes to life?' he questioned. 'I don't know magic.'

Devlin raised his hands again. 'You don't need to know magic, sire, I will enchant them for you.'

He intoned the harsh, unfamiliar words of the old magic once more and the snakes' frantic hissing calmed, their heads slowing then no longer straining to reach Valiant.

Devlin turned and bowed. 'The snakes are now under your command. They will do anything you tell them to do.'

An unpleasant smile flickered at the corner of Valiant's lips. 'Anything?'

'Just say the word.' Devlin grinned, revealing yellowing, crooked teeth.

Valiant stepped back, pointing at the sorcerer. '*Kill him!*' he snapped.

Devlin's smile was still on his lips when the first snake lunged at him, sinking its fangs into the flesh of his neck. The scream had barely started to build in his throat when the two remaining snakes joined in the attack.

Robert Mayer watched as the cloaked knight swept out of the village in a flurry of spray. As the sound of hoof beats faded into the night, he made his way through the deserted market to the stall of Devlin the sorcerer. The entire village had heard the scream, but somehow it had fallen to Mayer to go and see what had happened. Gingerly he drew aside the flaps covering Devlin's stall and peered into the dim interior.

Devlin lay sprawled across the earthen floor, his face frozen in an expression of pure terror, his hands out-stretched towards some unseen horror.

Mayer shook his head. He had disliked the sorcerer, but this was no way for a man to die. It was as he had said, nothing good ever happened when strangers came asking for Devlin.

Valiant rode through the night, the shield strapped securely to his arm. As the storm started to fade and early rays of light began to creep above the hills, he caught his first glimpse of his destination.

The vast castle spread out across the hillside. Flags and pennants fluttered from every tower, vivid and proud against the pale morning sky. Hundreds of buildings nestled within the protective walls, bathed in the light reflected off the gleaming white stone.

Spurring his horse onwards, Valiant entered the city gates, purposefully moving through the throng of horses, knights and officials that had started to gather for the tournament. He always liked to make an impression when he entered a city for the first time and his jet black horse and billowing, mustard-yellow cloak were already attracting attention. By keeping his helmet on he also conjured a sense of unease.

Eager servants hurried forward to steady his horse as he dismounted. Valiant barely acknowledged them. He strode across the field where the visiting knights were congregating at the desk of the steward, and stood impatiently as a competing knight clad in the colours of one of the eastern countries was registered by the court official.

'Store your amour and weapons in the armoury and report back here for the opening ceremony at nine o'clock tomorrow morning,' the official said finally.

The eastern knight nodded, then turned to leave, acknowledging Valiant with a curt bow of his head.

The steward looked up expectantly. Valiant lifted off his helmet and brought it down hard on the desk, making the official jump. With a humourless smile Valiant presented his colours: three black snakes on a blaze of yellow.

'Knight Valiant of the Western Isles,' he announced loudly.

The steward examined the proffered emblem carefully, then scratched the details in his ledger with a long quill.

'Welcome to Camelot.'

Chapter Two

The Grand Tournament of Camelot was one of the most eagerly anticipated weeks of the year. From far and wide, from neighbouring kingdoms and from across distant seas, people had been steadily gathering for several weeks, the atmosphere gradually building to fever pitch.

Every night the taverns were full to bursting, the patrons arguing animatedly about which knight had the best chance of winning. Wagers were made, sides were taken and arguments often spilled out into the street in rowdy tangles, swiftly dispersed by the palace guards.

Each new knight who arrived was met by a sea of eager faces, cheering and shouting, and a steady stream of officials, sternly intent on ensuring that they were properly registered for the event. The walls of the castle were alive with pennants and flags from dozens of kingdoms, the banqueting halls and royal chambers ablaze with torches night after night as King Uther Pendragon greeted each arrival in turn.

Traders and salesmen of dozens of different nationalities had set up their stalls outside the castle walls, each jostling with the other for the custom of the excited crowds. For the inhabitants of Camelot and the villagers from the surrounding districts, it was a chance to buy goods and trinkets from far distant lands, to sample food and drink that they had never dreamed of. Trade was almost as important as the tournament itself.

Preparing the grand arena had kept the labourers and craftsmen of Camelot busy for weeks, flattening the earth on which the battles would play out and erecting the stands for the audience. Slowly the structure had taken shape in the field outside the castle gates, the labourers watched day after day by excited, eager children. Positioned on one side of the stands was the scoreboard – a tall wooden frame studded with pegs on which the colours of the competing knights would be hung, only to be removed one by one as knights were defeated, the victors being moved up to the next tier.

On the other side of the arena another field had been designated as a preparation area for the competing knights; a low stable building had been converted into a temporary armoury and there were small tents for each competitor. Camelot's tournament was popular because of the simplicity of its premise: the challenge was simply knight versus knight, on foot, hand-to-hand, with the ancient weapons of battle, the sword and scimitar, blade against blade. It was the way that Uther Pendragon liked it: battle stripped down to its most basic level, a simple test of strength and skill, not dressed up in any way. It made the tournament brutal and dangerous, and the victory all the more desirable.

Over the years Camelot's tournament had become increasingly popular, drawing more and more knights to the kingdom to compete. This year there were enough entrants to keep the crowds entertained for nearly a week and each of the arrivals had one goal – to be proclaimed the overall champion.

Blacksmiths had been toiling well into the evenings to ensure that no knight would be without a weapon come the day, and smithy walls were heavy with gleaming swords and shining armour, while servants hurried to and fro collecting spare weapons constructed to their master's unique specifications. The fights put great strain on the sword blades, and no one wanted to be left with inferior weapons on the day.

Many of the older boys of the lower town had been

recruited as servants for the occasion. For weeks now they had been schooled in the rules of the tournament and the duties that the visiting knights would expect them to fulfil. Almost all would be placed with those visiting knights who were unable to bring their own entourage with them, whilst an unlucky few would be held back in the eventuality of sickness amongst the servants to Camelot's own knights.

There was intense rivalry amongst the boys, each of them wearing the emblem of their allocated knight like a badge of honour. For them, failure in their duties was tantamount to failure in the arena.

After the knights of Camelot, it was the eastern knights who had the greatest following. With their curved swords and richly decorated tunics and cloaks, they seemed exotic and mysterious and to be placed in their service was considered a great honour.

The highest honour, however, was to be awarded the role of servant to the reigning champion, a task given even more importance this year because the current champion was Uther Pendragon's own son, Prince Arthur. Amongst the servants, it had been a source of angry conversation and bitter disappointment that Arthur's latest servant was hardly ideal for the position.

★

The morning sun had just cleared the treetops, bathing the walls of Camelot in soft yellow light. Arthur Pendragon stood tall in the training fields, stretching and feeling the warmth of the sun on his back. The air was filled with the sound of sword blades clashing and the bellows of the knights as they practised. The noise gave Arthur goose bumps, though he wasn't sure if that was excitement at the thought of the impending tournament or apprehension at the expectations of the court.

He had had to sit through another of his father's speeches about honour and chivalry again at breakfast, of the role of the knight, and how the reputation of the royal name of Pendragon would rest upon his shoulders in the coming days. It had not put Arthur in the best of moods.

His mood became sourer as his sparring partner emerged from inside the castle.

Merlin.

Arthur felt himself flush with anger and embarrassment. Of all the people who could have been placed as his servant, Merlin was the absolute worst. And at such a vital time too! He had tried to talk his father out of it, but Uther Pendragon was having none of it. In his eyes

Merlin had already proved himself by saving his son's life from the treachery of an evil witch; placing him at Arthur's side was right and proper.

Arthur twirled his sword angrily. He still wasn't sure quite how Merlin had managed to engineer matters so that he had looked so heroic, but Arthur was certain of one thing – he was going to make Merlin regret every day spent in his service.

Merlin staggered out onto the fields, his lanky frame weighed down by the training armour that he had been supplied with. He tugged at the front of the ill-fitting breastplate. Arthur's previous servant had been considerably wider in girth, and even though Merlin had pulled the straps as tight as they would go, the armour still hung off him. He really wasn't sure how much protection it was going to give him; at the moment it just seemed to be sliding around every time he moved.

He stared across at where Arthur Pendragon twirled his sword in the early morning light. Arthur was determined to get in as much practice as he could before tomorrow. Unfortunately, practice meant that he had to have someone to practise *with*, and with all the other knights and servants concentrating on their own tournament strategies, that someone was Merlin.

The prince's sword stabbed down into the hard earth and Arthur leaned on the hilt, peering at Merlin.

'Ready?'

Merlin gave a nervous smile. 'Would it make any difference if I said no?'

Arthur shook his head. 'Not really.'

Merlin barely had time to slip the oversized helmet onto his head and raise his shield before Arthur swung his sword in a wide arc. Merlin could feel vibrations shudder through his entire body as the blow connected.

With each swing of his sword Arthur called out, trying to get Merlin to parry.

'Shield! Body! Shield!'

Merlin flailed wildly with his shield as blow after blow rained down on him.

'Body! Shield!' cried Arthur. 'Come on, I've got a tournament to win! You're not even *trying*!'

Merlin staggered backwards, vainly trying to ward off blows, but the sword was so heavy he could barely lift it and the huge helmet kept sliding down over his eyes, obscuring Arthur from view.

'Helmet!'

A sudden blow to the side of his head sent him reeling one way. Before he could even regain his balance, another blow to the other side of his helmet sent him staggering back the other way. His foot slipped on the dew-soaked grass and he toppled backwards with a crash, his helmet rolling away.

As Merlin lay on his back staring at the blue of the sky and wondering why everything seemed to be swirling, Arthur's face loomed over him, nodding approvingly, his mood clearly brightened by Merlin's demonstration of his skill.

'You're braver than you look. Most servants collapse after the first few blows.'

'Oh, great. That's good to know.' Merlin tried to focus, shaking his head to try and clear the ringing. 'So, is it over?'

Arthur gave a sly smile. 'That was just the warm-up.' He held up a spiked ball on a long chain. 'How's your mace work coming along?'

Merlin let his head thump back onto the grass. He was never to going to survive until lunch time.

Arthur watched as Merlin staggered back to his feet and went to retrieve his helmet. Despite himself the prince had to admit that he was surprised at how well Merlin had stood up to the bout. Arthur had been unnecessarily hard on him, fully expecting him to be out for the count after the first few blows. Not only had Merlin taken the beating without complaint, but he was actually prepared to carry on. Perhaps he wasn't the total waste of space that he had at first seemed to be.

Groaning, Merlin bent down and picked up the battered and dented helmet. With a resigned look over at Arthur, he slipped the helmet back onto his head and hefted the shield onto his arm.

Arthur raised his mace.

'Let's see how long you can keep going this time,' he murmured.

Merlin stumbled down the long, flagstoned corridor of the servants' quarters. All around him people bustled to and fro with plates piled high with food prepared for the next day's tournament feast. The air was full of the smells of roasting meats, spiced ales and baking breads.

At the end of the corridor was a steep, narrow spiral staircase. A sign hanging on the wall read: *Court Physician*. Merlin climbed the stairs, wincing at every step. At the top was a heavy wooden door. He pushed it open and stumbled gratefully into the musty, cinnamon-scented calm of Gaius' chambers.

The room was large and gloomy, lit by shafts of light that lanced down from windows high in the curving stone walls and by dozens of torches dotted around the place. Bookcases and cupboards were squeezed into every alcove, each one bulging under the weight of books and bottles. A low bed was tucked against a far wall.

Gaius was huddled over the huge wooden table that dominated the room, decanting drops of vivid purple liquid into a collection of large glass bottles. He was an old man, his long grey hair hanging in unruly strands over his simple robes. He looked up as Merlin entered.

'So, how was your first day as Arthur's servant?' he asked.

Merlin squinted at him, tapping the side of his head with the palm of his hand.

'Can you hear clanging?' he said as he tried to flatten his hair which was sticking out wildly from his head. He wasn't sure if he would ever hear anything other than ringing in his ears for the rest of his life. His breastplate had slipped so that it was hanging down over his waist and somehow he'd managed to get one of his leg shields twisted around so that it was facing the wrong way.

Gaius got up and guided Merlin to one of the low stools that dotted the room. Merlin groaned as the old physician started to rub at the knots in his aching shoulders.

'I'm certain that it couldn't have been that bad,' said Gaius.

'It was horrible!' protested Merlin. 'No, it was worse than horrible. *Merlin, do this, Merlin, do that, Merlin, stand there whilst I whack you around the head with a sword.*'

Gaius grimaced. He had tended to several of Arthur's servants in the past and knew the damage that these 'practice' bouts could inflict. The difference was that Arthur's previous servant, Morris, had been considerably sturdier than Merlin, and even he had ended up in the physician's chambers on more than one occasion. He would have to stock up on his healing balms and ointments.

'Sounds painful.'

'Trust me! It was! I haven't stopped running around all day and I've still got to learn all about tournament etiquette by tomorrow morning.'

Merlin glanced across at a large leather-bound tome lying at the far end of the table. From amongst the hundreds of books that lined the walls of Gaius' chambers, he had found a book about the duties expected of a knight's manservant, and the rules and regulations of a tournament.

Well, perhaps *found* wasn't quite the right word, but then it was hardly his fault if Gaius' filing system was less than efficient. It would have taken hours, perhaps even days, of searching if he hadn't made use of his rather special talents.

He stretched out his hand towards the book and muttered a series of harsh, alien words under his breath, feeling the familiar warmth building in his head. His eyes flared with a glittering, golden glow and the book slid across the table towards him, pages flipping open to the place where Merlin had been reading over breakfast. The page showed a diagram of a knight's armour.

Exasperated, Gaius clouted him hard across the back of the head.

'What have I told you about using magic like that?'

Merlin winced. He knew that the old physician was right. He felt safe in Gaius' rooms, and that was making him careless. 'If I could actually feel my arms then I'd pick up the book myself!' he complained.

'Never mind your arms.' Gaius glared at him. 'What am I going to do if you get caught?'

Merlin glanced up at him, a quizzical eyebrow raised. 'What *would* you do?'

The two stared at each other for a moment, both well aware of the consequences if Uther Pendragon ever learned that sorcery was being practised within the walls of Camelot, let alone what he would do if he discovered that a young sorcerer was actually living under his protection. On his first day in Camelot, Merlin had seen for himself the fate awaiting anyone using magic. He felt a knot in the pit of his stomach as he remembered the dull thud that the executioner's axe had made as it fell.

'You just make sure that it doesn't happen,' said Gaius sternly. 'For both our sakes.'

Merlin nodded and picked up the book, trying to shake the unpleasant image of the execution from his mind. There were pages of rules and regulations that he was meant to memorize, and details of the duties that he was meant to perform. It was complicated. Confusing.

And dull.

He slumped back in his chair, letting the book thump down onto the table.

'I save Arthur from being killed and I end up as his servant. How is that fair?'

Gaius shrugged. It was true that without Merlin's intervention Arthur would have met an unpleasant end at the hands of a witch, Mary Collins, but to have revealed the true extent of Merlin's involvement would have meant exposing his magical abilities. Besides, as far as Uther was concerned, awarding Merlin the position of Arthur's manservant was a great honour.

'I'm not sure that fairness comes into it.' Gaius gave

Merlin's arm a sharp tug, stretching the muscles. 'You never know, it might be fun.'

Merlin gasped with pain and looked up at him in disbelief. 'You think that mucking out Arthur's horses is going to be fun? You should see my list of duties!'

Gaius shrugged. 'We all have duties. Even Arthur.'

'Oh, yeah.' Merlin gave a snort of contempt. 'It must be so tough for him. All the girls, and the glory, and the trophies. And more girls. Poor old Arthur.'

'He is the future king!' said Gaius impatiently. 'Everyone expects so much of him. He's under a lot of pressure.'

Merlin winced as Gaius gave his aching shoulder another squeeze. 'That makes two of us!'

Chapter Three

The following morning Merlin made his way into the lower town that nestled beneath Camelot's protective walls. After a fruitless night spent trying to make some sense of the armour diagrams in his book, he had dropped into an uneasy sleep filled with dreams of Arthur stepping out onto the tournament field without a single piece of armour tied in the correct place. It seemed so stupid that he couldn't use magic to accomplish in minutes what was liable to take him hours.

Waking early, Merlin had gathered up all the disparate pieces of Arthur's suit of armour and gone to find the one person who might be able to help him make sense of things.

Staggering under the weight, he tottered through the town. There were so many people around! He had known that the tournament was popular, but he had had no idea that it would be such a big event. Everywhere he looked there were pennants and flags hanging from windows and rooftops and the chatter of everyone around him seemed to be about nothing else. Young men had fashioned themselves crude representations of the colours of the knights that they were supporting and small children dashed about with wooden swords, competing in noisy tournaments of their own.

Merlin remembered a day several years ago when some of the men from his village had decided that they would come to the tournament. Merlin had been too young to join them at the time, not that his mother would have let him go anyway – she was always too worried that he might inadvertently reveal his gift in a moment of excitement. He recalled watching the men set off along the road to Camelot, laughing and teasing each other. He had been sad at the time. Not about missing the tournament itself – Merlin had never seen the point of watching grown men doing their level best to try and injure each other – but about not seeing Camelot. Now, only a short time later, here he was living in the castle itself.

As he passed one of the taverns, half a dozen young men, already rowdy and reeking of ale despite the early hour, caught sight of the armour that he carried and started to cheer and chant noisily.

One of them staggered over to him, pointing at the emblem of Pendragon emblazoned on the armour. 'He carries the colours of the champion!' he cried, catching Merlin by the arm. 'Come and join us, lad. If you are the servant to our champion then you're a friend of ours.' The stumbling man tried to drag him towards the tavern, but Merlin managed to extricate himself pretty easily from his fumbling grip.

'I'm sorry. I've got a lot to do . . .'

'Quite right too . . .' The man slumped down on the bench next to his friends. 'We wouldn't want to keep you from your duties.' He leaned forward conspiratorially. 'Don't ever let my good lady wife find out, but I've put my entire week's wages on Prince Arthur winning this tournament. You look after him, lad. You make sure that you send him out there well placed to win this for us. We're relying on you, aren't we, lads?'

The men started to sing again as Merlin hurried away. The young men might be relying on him, but Merlin knew that far more was at stake here than a few bets. Arthur himself wouldn't give him a moment's rest until he was performing like a proper servant – his expectations, and demands, were high. But if he were to tie a piece of armour badly, or let Arthur down in some other way . . . well, the prince's life could be forfeit. His safety, literally, was in Merlin's hands.

He kept remembering, too, what the Great Dragon had told him – that Arthur was the '*once and future king who will unite the land of Albion*'. That was Arthur's destiny. And to be by the prince's side was Merlin's, as the Dragon had made clear: '*Without you, Arthur will never succeed. Without you, there will be no Albion.*' Like it or not, Merlin knew he had to protect the prince. At whatever cost. This tournament was just the beginning.

It was a weighty responsibility . . .

He hurried down the street to the smithy, though it wasn't Tom the blacksmith that he was here to see; it was his daughter. Pushing the door open with his aching shoulder, Merlin peered inside. Guinevere was sweeping up the workshop floor. She looked up with a smile as Merlin entered.

'Merlin!'

Merlin grinned back. Of all the people he had met since he had arrived in Camelot, Gwen was one of his favourites. She was the maidservant of the king's ward, the Lady Morgana, but she had none of the snootiness of some of the other palace staff. Plus she was one of the few people who didn't think that he was anything special, but who liked him anyway. She was, well, normal, for want of a better word, and someone who he could call a friend.

Merlin held out the pieces of armour and looked at her pleadingly.

'Help?'

A short time later Merlin stood in the centre of the smithy, fully clad in Arthur's tournament armour, unsurprisingly not quite managing to look as regal or as poised as Arthur usually did. In fact, Merlin wasn't even sure how Arthur managed to walk in this, let alone fight! No wonder he was so concerned about his servant being properly trained.

Gwen was telling him for what seemed like the hundredth time the names of the various parts of the armour and in what order they had to be put on.

'So, you've got the voiders on the arms, the hauberk goes over your chest, and I guess you know what to do with the helmet?'

Merlin grinned. 'That was the only bit I'd figured out!' He looked at her with admiration in his eyes. 'How come you're so much better at this than me?'

Gwen shrugged. 'I'm a blacksmith's daughter. I know

pretty much everything there is to know about armour.'
She sighed. 'Which is actually kind of sad.'

'No,' said Merlin, smiling widely. 'It's brilliant!'

Gwen's face lit up with pleasure, then just as quickly
she blushed, dropping her eyes from Merlin's.

'It suits you. You look like a knight.'

'Really?' Merlin peered at his reflection in one of the
many shields and breastplates that lined the walls.

Guinevere picked up the hem of her apron and
curtsied. 'It's a pleasure to meet you, Knight Merlin.'

Grinning, Merlin grabbed a sword, brandishing it
high over his head. 'I fight for your honour, my Lady
Guinevere.' He swung the sword enthusiastically, forgetting for a moment the dozens of metal goods hanging
from the smithy rafters.

There was a deafening clatter as the sword caught on
the handle of a large tankard, flinging it from the nail on
which it hung and sending it flying.

At the same moment the door on the far side of the
workshop swung open and a very surprised-looking
blacksmith ducked as the tankard bounced off the
lintel.

He stooped and picked up the makeshift missile.
Merlin grimaced as he caught sight of the dent that his
inelegant swordsmanship had caused.

'Merlin, this is Tom, my father.' Gwen hurried over to him and gave him a peck on the cheek. 'Father, this is Merlin, Arthur's new servant.'

Tom nodded at him. 'Nice to meet you, Merlin.' He ran a calloused finger over the dent that Merlin's sword had made. 'Even if you did damage my favourite tankard.'

Merlin gave a nervous smile. 'Sorry about that.'

Gwen caught hold of her father's arm and pulled him over to Merlin, desperate to change the subject. 'I was helping him out with Arthur's armour.'

Tom looked at the expertly tied straps and buckles appreciatively. 'So I see. So, Merlin, ready for the big day?'

'I hope so.' Merlin gingerly put the sword he had borrowed onto the workbench. 'Actually, I'd better get over to the arena.' He struggled to unfasten the buckle on the back of the hauberk – but he couldn't quite reach it. Keen to get out from under the amused gaze of Gwen's father, he tried unsuccessfully to slide the breast-plate over his head.

Gwen stifled a laugh as Merlin contorted and twisted until he eventually gave up. He looked at her pleadingly.

'How do you get out of this thing?'

★

Merlin hurried towards the tournament arena with a new spring in his step. He finally felt that he might actually be able to fulfil his duties. He'd show Arthur that he wasn't so useless after all . . .

He kept running though the names of the various pieces of armour, reminding himself of what Gwen had taught him.

'Voiders, hauberk. Voiders, hauberk . . .'

'Merlin.'

He looked up. It was Arthur's old servant, Morris. He had been less than pleased when he had been dismissed from being the prince's principal servant and replaced by someone who barely knew his way around the castle. The timing couldn't have been worse either. Being dismissed within weeks of the tournament starting had been the cause of much embarrassment and teasing for Morris. Merlin felt sorry for him. It wasn't as if he had *wanted* to be given the job of Arthur's manservant − in fact he had done his best to try and wriggle out of it − but the king had been having none of it. Merlin had tried to avoid bumping into Morris since then.

Morris eyed the armour piled up in Merlin's arms and Merlin was suddenly aware of all the fingerprints and scuffmarks that he hadn't got around to cleaning off yet.

'I'm just on my way to get some polish,' he blurted out.

Morris shook his head in despair. 'Just make sure you don't forget to fasten the vambrace.'

Merlin watched him make his way through the village with a sinking heart.

'What's a vambrace? She didn't say anything about a *vambrace*!'

Chapter Four

The meeting with Morris had thrown Merlin's confidence, and by the time he arrived at the tournament field he was struggling to remember anything that Gwen had told him.

He'd thought that he'd started well, but as he finished securing the last buckle on Arthur's right leg, he suddenly realized that the piece of armour that he had just secured should have been on his right *arm* instead.

It all went downhill from there as Merlin hurried to try and correct his mistakes, getting increasingly flustered as he watched knight after knight stride out into the arena, their perfectly assembled armour glinting in the morning light.

Arthur, too, had noticed the steady stream of combatants. At this rate he was going to be the last out onto the field.

'You do know that the tournament starts today?' he snapped.

'Yes, sire.' Merlin strained to shut the clasp on Arthur's backplate. 'I'm aware of that.'

There was a sharp click as the backplate finally snapped into place. Merlin gave a sigh of relief. All that remained were the helmet and gauntlets; even he couldn't muck those up.

Taking a quick glance over Arthur's shoulder, Merlin saw the bustle of eager crowds now making their way to the stands. It seemed as though everyone in Camelot was turning out to watch the tournament. Messengers, their court garments bright and gaudy, hurried through the mêlée of peasants and courtiers. Guards, their own armour shining in the bright morning sun, stared down attentively from their prime viewpoints high on the castle walls. Everyone was looking forward to the day's events.

Well, nearly everyone. Gaius had also been up early, preparing a bag packed with bandages and lotions and herbs, muttering under his breath about 'overgrown schoolboys playing at soldiers'.

Smiling to himself, Merlin picked up Arthur's heavy gauntlets from the table and handed them to the prince. 'That is one seriously big crowd.'

Arthur shot him a filthy look. Merlin realized with a jolt of surprise that Arthur was quite unsettled by the size of the audience he was attracting. Merlin had assumed that the prince would love all the glamour and attention of the tournament, the brashness and unsubtlety of the visiting knights, the false posturing and bravado. But there was nothing that said that in Arthur's face; instead, he seemed disturbed, anxious. Merlin felt a pang of guilt. He was certain that his ineptitude in preparing the prince for battle couldn't be helping at all.

'You nervous?' he asked.

'I don't get nervous.' Arthur snatched the gauntlets from him.

'Really?' Merlin shrugged and helped the prince struggle into the heavy chain-mail gloves. 'I thought everyone got nervous.'

'Will you shut up!' snapped Arthur.

Merlin bit his lip. Once again, his uncanny knack of saying precisely the wrong thing at precisely the wrong time had got him into trouble. He quickly picked up Arthur's cloak, slipping it over the prince's head and tying it with an inelegant knot. He grabbed the helmet from the table, thrust it into the prince's arms and stood back, nodding appreciatively.

'OK, great, you're all set . . .' He paused, unsure of what a servant should say at this point.

Arthur stared at him in disbelief.

'Aren't you forgetting something?'

Merlin's face fell. He stared around him frantically. Surely he couldn't have missed anything. There were the voiders, the hauberk, the vambrace . . .

'My sword!' yelled Arthur.

Groaning with embarrassment, Merlin hurried to remove the sword from its stand. 'Right. Sorry. I guess you'll be needing that.'

Arthur snatched the sword from him impatiently and strode out towards the arena, barely giving Merlin a second glance.

Merlin gave a sigh. 'Well, that went well . . .'

Arthur marched away from his servant, unsure if he was angry because Merlin had proved to be so utterly useless or because he had managed to gauge so accurately how he was feeling.

Why couldn't he just stay silent? That's what servants were supposed to be – silent, dutiful and obedient. Instead, Merlin had opened up all manner of feelings that Arthur had hoped would remain buried. He closed his eyes for a moment, trying to regain his focus, his composure, ready to face the gaze of both his public and his father.

Taking a deep breath, Prince Arthur stepped into the arena.

The tournament arena was a wide circle of bare earth ringed with tiers of wooden benches. Flags and pennants fluttered high overhead, everything in the red and yellow colours of Camelot, while peasants and courtiers alike jostled for the best seats and court officials hurried to ensure that all was prepared for the first round.

In the centre of the stands was the high-backed throne of Uther Pendragon, beside which the king himself stood expectantly, watching carefully as the knights started to assemble before him.

He was a tall man, broad-chested and straight-backed, his entire bearing honed by years of battle. From beneath the band of burnished gold that encircled his head, a faint line cut across his forehead – a blemish on his handsome features but an obvious reminder that this was a warrior as well as a king.

At the front of the royal stands sat his ward, the Lady Morgana, her raven hair and shimmering fur-trimmed gown as much a part of the spectacle as the knights and bustle of the arena. Next to her sat Guinevere, finished with her chores at the smithy and now fulfilling her duties as Morgana's maidservant. They, too, were inspecting the assembled knights, though with somewhat different motives.

'This is brilliant,' whispered Gwen conspiratorially.

Morgana suppressed a smile. Gwen hadn't attended a tournament before; the excitement would soon start to wane as the fights blurred one into another. She cast her knowledgeable eye over the two dozen or so young men lined up before her. Children playing at being men. Her eye was drawn to a strongly built, rugged knight with close-cropped hair and piercing grey eyes. He seemed different, holding his place with an arrogant ease that made him stand out from the rest. She leaned towards Gwen with a slight frown. 'Who is that?'

'That's Knight Valiant,' Gwen murmured. 'I've heard that he's amazing.'

Morgana glanced briefly towards where Arthur was taking his place at the end of the line. He had been insufferable for most of the week, boasting about how he was certain to win the tournament again and complaining at how he would be forced to escort Morgana to the feast on the last night of the proceedings. Despite his princely status, he was just like all the other knights of Camelot – vain and childish, too eager to try and score points. He was a good-looking boy, that much was true, but Valiant looked a man, a battleworn, mysterious man. She hoped that he would prove to be an interesting adversary for the prince.

Valiant suddenly looked up, as if aware of the girls' eyes on him. He flashed them a dazzling smile and bowed low.

'Did you see that?' Gwen's eyes registered delight.

Morgana said nothing, merely flicked a strand of jet black hair from her eyes. She was aware that her heart was beating rather faster than it had been.

Knight Valiant was gorgeous.

Valiant smiled inwardly as the Lady Morgana broke off her gaze, twirling her hair and whispering with her maidservant. He had heard tales of the beauty of Uther Pendragon's ward, but had been unprepared for quite how stunning she was in the flesh. She could be an added bonus.

A triumphant fanfare brought his attention back to the tournament. A dozen trumpets cut through the chatter of the crowd, bringing silence to the arena.

Uther Pendragon turned to the expectant knights lined before him.

'Knights of the realm,' his voice boomed out, strong

and confident. 'It's a great honour to welcome you to Camelot's tournament. Over the coming days you will put your bravery and your skills as warriors to the test and, of course, challenge the reigning champion – my son, Prince Arthur.'

Valiant stared down the line at the young prince. This was the so-called unbeatable champion that he had come here to fight. He had already checked his name on the tournament scoreboard. Whether it was by luck or by fate, he and the prince were on opposite sides of the draw, so he would need to make it to the final if he was to face Arthur Pendragon in battle – to the ultimate bout that would take place on the last day of the tournament.

Arthur's reputed skill as a swordsman should ensure that he reached the final.

The shield was Valiant's guarantee that he, too, would progress that far.

Arthur caught his gaze and stared back at him, as if sensing the challenge. The two men locked eyes for what seemed like an age, then, with a small bow of his head, Valiant looked away, turning his attention to the king once more.

'Only one can have the honour of being crowned champion – and he will receive a prize of one thousand gold pieces,' boomed Uther.

A girl with long golden hair stepped forward, a wooden box cradled in her arms. Even though the girl was almost as beautiful as Morgana, Valiant only had eyes for what the box contained. This was the other reason for his presence here at Camelot and his overriding desire to win. Gold. More gold than he could ever want. He had heard rumours that Camelot held a vast amount of treasure in its vaults, spoils from the war twenty years ago against the Dragons. From the look of the gold pieces that glittered in the wooden box those rumours were true.

'It is in combat that we learn a knight's true nature.' Uther's gaze flickered to his son. 'Whether he is indeed a warrior, or a coward.'

From the corner of his eye, Valiant saw a frown flicker across Arthur Pendragon's brow. Was the boy nervous? Worried about disappointing his father, his king? It would be unsurprising, given his father's reputation as a knight. Valiant smiled inwardly. That was a weakness, and one that he could use to his advantage.

Uther spread his arms wide. 'Let the tournament begin!'

The knights raised their swords in salute and the crowd roared their appreciation. Valiant drank in the applause. This was what he lived for – the appreciation of the crowd and the glory of battle. As he filed out with his fellow combatants, Valiant watched as the first two knights to fight – Prince Arthur and Sir Alfred – approached the king, presenting their colours and preparing for their bout.

Uther leaned towards his son. 'I trust you will make me proud,' he muttered.

Valiant saw a frown crease Arthur's brow once more. The boy *was* nervous. He just hoped that those nerves didn't fail him before the final. Defeating the prince was his right, his destiny, and he wasn't going to be cheated of it by some lesser knight. Taking his place in the preparation area, he waited with eager anticipation for the fight to begin.

Merlin watched as Uther took his seat in the stands and Arthur and Alfred took to the centre of the arena to the cheers and whoops of the crowd. Despite himself Merlin suddenly found that he felt nervous on the prince's behalf. What would the crowd think if Arthur was beaten in the very first round?

Merlin dismissed the thought. Sir Alfred was a good swordsman, but not *that* good. Besides, he knew that Arthur had beaten Alfred easily in the previous tournament. He would do the same this year.

At least, he would, just so long as his armour had been fastened correctly . . .

Fingers crossed, Merlin watched as the two knights saluted each other across the field, then pulled on their helmets. For a moment the two men paused, watching each other intently, then with a burst of movement, they both launched themselves forward.

To the roar of the crowd, the two knights clashed in a whirl of sword blades. Merlin's jaw dropped at the speed at which the two men moved in the heavy armour.

Alfred swung his sword in a series of lightning moves but Arthur parried each one effortlessly, spinning on the balls of his feet and dancing out of reach of the slicing blade. Then he launched his own attack, delivering a dozen crushing blows to Alfred's shield that sent him reeling.

Merlin gave a gasp of appreciation and, finding himself unexpectedly caught up in the atmosphere, bellowed, 'Go on!' urging Arthur forward.

The fight was over in a matter of moments. Alfred made a brave attempt to parry the prince's blows, but in the end his swordsmanship was just not up to Arthur's standard. As Alfred's colours were removed from the scoreboard and the emblem of Pendragon was transferred to the second tier, Arthur looked up triumphantly, acknowledging the deafening cheers of the crowd. Merlin found himself applauding along with them.

Throughout the rest of the day, bout after bout brought thunderous appreciation from the assembled crowd. Knights from across the realm fought long and hard to reach the next round. Whilst everyone in their crowd had their favourites in each contest, two names constantly found favour with the cheering mob: Arthur and Valiant.

Merlin and Arthur watched from the preparation area as Valiant dispatched yet another opponent, winning the last fight of the day and drinking in the adulation of the people of Camelot.

'Knight Valiant looks pretty handy with a sword,' said Merlin, struggling to remove Arthur's battered breastplate.

Arthur nodded. The knight was indeed an impressive swordsman. But not so great, he felt sure, that one of the more experienced knights of Camelot wouldn't be able to defeat him. He was about to say so to Merlin when Valiant strode into the preparation area. Casting his helmet aside, he nodded curtly at Arthur. 'May

I offer you my congratulations on your victories today.'

'Likewise.' Arthur studied the man carefully. There was something not quite right about this knight, something that he couldn't quite put his finger on, but his father seemed to appreciate his somewhat coarse fighting style and that meant even more pressure to perform well in the following day's contests.

'I hope to see you at the reception this evening.' Valiant bowed his head and strode off.

Merlin made a face at his retreating back. 'Creep.'

For a moment Arthur was tempted to clap Merlin on the back. It was just what he had been thinking. Valiant *was* a creep, and it hadn't taken Merlin long to work that out. He turned away to stop his servant seeing the smile on his face. Even though he agreed with Merlin it was hardly right for a servant to talk that way about a knight of the realm, or for a prince to encourage him. He plucked up his grime-encrusted shield, looking at the scars that cut across the royal crest. There was a lot to get done by tomorrow.

Or rather, there was a lot for *Merlin* to get done by tomorrow. Whether he was right about Valiant or not, it wasn't going to get him out of his duties. He thrust the shield at Merlin.

'For tomorrow, you need to repair my shield, wash my tunic, clean my boots, sharpen my sword, polish my chain mail . . .'

Merlin paled as the list of tasks got longer, and longer, and longer.

Chapter Five

Merlin lay back on his bed, absorbed in the book on magic and sorcery that Gaius had given him on one of his first days in Camelot. The tasks that Arthur had given him were being accomplished with methodical precision, and with considerably less effort than expected.

Merlin let the book drop and gazed admiringly at his handiwork. All around the room various pieces of armour were being attended to. Floating by the window was a pair of boots, the brush that cleaned them dipping to the jar of polish on the floor like some bizarre seabird diving for a fish. Across the room, a hammer darted to and fro around the breastplate, hammering out dents whilst a cloth buffed the metal to a high shine. The sword ran its length back and forth in a perfect line across a sharpening stone, whilst Arthur's sweat-soaked tunic dipped in and out of a bucket of water before wringing itself out and flapping about to dry itself in the breeze.

Merlin nodded in satisfaction. *This* was how magic should be used. Surely no one could find the slightest harm in using sorcery to handle dull, monotonous tasks. Besides, he had done his fair share of hard work today. When he had returned to Gaius' chambers, he had felt exhilarated, buoyed up by the festival atmosphere of the tournament. He had even felt relatively pleased with himself about how he had performed his various duties. He was certain that he had turned out to be a better servant than Arthur had expected, and despite the long list of things that needed to be accomplished by morning the prince hadn't quite been the odious taskmaster that Merlin had been dreading.

'Merlin!'

Gaius' voice called out and Merlin could hear footsteps on the short flight of steps that led up to his room. Panicking, Merlin shoved the magic book under his pillow and clicked his fingers at the swarm of hovering cleaning implements. '*Gestillan!*' he breathed, his eyes blazing. Everything came to a sudden halt as the door swung open and Gaius stared suspiciously into the room.

'Are you using magic again?'

Merlin tried to put on his best innocent expression. 'No.'

There was a deafening clatter as all the pieces of armour, brushes, hammers and articles of clothing crashed to the floor in an untidy pile.

Gaius glared at him. 'What's all this then?'

Merlin said nothing. He had been caught red-handed.

Gaius shook his head in despair.

'I just came to tell you that dinner's ready.'

On the other side of the castle, in the grand throne room, a great reception was taking place. The meats and pastries and finery that had previously crowded the tables of the palace kitchens were now spread generously across the long banqueting tables that lined the room. Torches on the walls and dozens of candles on every table cast flickering pools of light on the flagstoned floor and gentle music drifted down from the minstrels' gallery.

Morgana looked around the bustling room with delight. She was always in her element at these events. After the tournament she and Gwen had spent the rest of the day choosing an appropriate gown for the evening. Well, perhaps appropriate wasn't quite the word for the dress that she had selected, but as far as Morgana was concerned, it was perfect for the effect she was trying to create.

She smiled to herself. Her guardian always insisted that she stood at his shoulder for the first hour or so. Normally Morgana endured these more formal parts of the evening with a certain amount of weary resignation; tonight, however, she had a very good reason to remain right by Uther's side.

At the end of the hall, courtiers were ushering the visiting knights into the throne room to be presented to the king. In stark contrast to the armour they had been wearing in the arena, they were now in their finest doublets and robes. They slowly made their way down a long line of waiting dignitaries who shook them enthusiastically by the hand, congratulating them on the battles of the day.

Morgana smiled politely as knight after knight tried to catch her eye or engage her in conversation. She was bored with their endless chatter about trivial subjects – and she was waiting to talk to the powerful-looking knight with piercing eyes towards the end of the line, hoping that his conversation would be as dynamic as his swordsmanship.

She smoothed down her dress as Valiant presented

himself to the king, watching him carefully as he bowed crisply and confidently.

'Knight Valiant of the Western Isles, my lord. I want to say what an honour it is to compete in your tournament.'

Uther clasped his hand firmly. 'I saw you fighting today. You have a very aggressive style.'

Valiant gave a modest shrug of his shoulders. 'As my lord said, it is combat that reveals a knight's true nature. To lose is to be disgraced.'

Uther nodded. 'I couldn't agree more.'

Morgana could tell that her guardian was almost as impressed by this knight as she was. Uther caught him by the arm and drew him in front of her.

'Knight Valiant, may I present Lady Morgana, my ward.'

Valiant bowed low as Uther turned back to the line of waiting knights. With her guardian's attention elsewhere, Morgana held out a slender hand. Valiant kissed it gently, his eyes never leaving her own.

'My lady.'

On the edge of her vision she could see Arthur glaring at her furiously. Good. It was about time he realized that he wasn't the only swordsman in the kingdom.

'I saw you competing today,' she said to the knight in front of her.

'And I saw you watching.' Valiant rose, still holding her hand. 'I understand that the tournament champion has the honour of escorting my lady to the feast?'

'That is correct.' Morgana flashed him her most dazzling smile.

'Then I would give anything to win the tournament.' Valiant released her hand, bowed and moved on to the next dignitary in line. Morgana stared after him. He really could turn out to be something special.

She was still thinking about the mysterious knight from the Western Isles when Arthur approached her. Morgana nodded over at where Valiant was making small talk with some of her guardian's advisors.

'They all seem to be rather impressed by Knight Valiant.'

'They're not the only ones.' The tone in Arthur's voice was unmistakable.

Morgana turned, raising her eyebrows, glad of an opportunity to tease him. 'What's the matter, Arthur? Not jealous, are you?'

Arthur looked her up and down. 'I can't see there's anything to be jealous of.' With a smirk on his lips, he walked off to join some of his fellow knights.

Morgana watched him go, her cheeks flushing with rage. Could Arthur be any more annoying? She doubted it. He was just a boy after all, childish and petty. She turned to Gwen.

'I hope Knight Valiant wins the tournament,' she said angrily.

Gwen shot her a concerned look. 'You don't really mean that?'

'Yes, I do.' Morgana glared over at where Arthur was laughing and joking with his friends.

Gaius placed the last of the dinner plates back on the rack in the small kitchen area of his chambers and sat down wearily in one of his high-backed chairs, glad to finally take the weight off his feet.

It had been a long day. The first days of a tournament were always busy as the more experienced knights quickly dispatched their less skilled opponents and moved on to the next round. Gaius had spent the day with a steady stream of patients, tending to cuts and bruises, to black eyes and sprained wrists. One of the younger knights had needed to have a broken finger put in a splint, but much to the knight's embarrassment it had actually been due to his catching his hand in one of the stable doors and nothing to do with his bout in the arena at all.

Unfortunately, things were unlikely to get any easier over the coming days. As the knights became more evenly matched, the bouts became longer and more aggressive and the injuries got considerably more serious. There had already been one near miss. One of Knight Valiant's opponents had been lucky to escape without a sword blade through his shoulder. Gaius frowned; despite all the cheering and encouragement of the crowd, he had found Valiant's style of fighting to be crude and vicious.

He gave a deep sigh. He was going to be very busy during the tournament.

Gaius glanced over at the door to Merlin's room. He had sent him off to bed after dinner. The boy was exhausted, but still determined to master the difficult servant's tasks that the prince had set him. Gaius smiled. They were an unlikely match those two – the handsome, athletic prince and the gangly, awkward sorcerer. Even though Merlin had only been in the castle a short time, Gaius had become incredibly fond of him. He was a bright, personable boy, already popular with many of the palace staff, and despite his complaints he had proved himself to be a diligent servant to the young prince.

Gaius frowned, remembering Merlin's use of magic before dinner and earlier in the day. The boy was becoming too casual about using his powers within the castle. Gaius understood how he must be feeling – to have had to hide his gift for so long must have been hard, and to finally find someone who he could talk to about it, someone who understood . . . One moment of carelessness was all that it would take, however, to bring terrible trouble down on both of them and Gaius wasn't sure that he could bear it if anything happened to Merlin.

He got up, rubbing his eyes wearily. He was being unfair. Merlin wasn't stupid. The boy was only too aware of what fate awaited those who practised magic; he had seen graphic evidence of that from the very first moment that he had set foot in Camelot.

Wincing at the pain in his protesting back, Gaius leaned over and blew out the candles that flickered on the table. From across the courtyard came the distant sound of laughter and loud conversation. Gaius shook his head.

'Drinking with each other one minute, beating each other around the head with swords the next,' he said wryly to himself. Then he sighed and, with weary expectations of the day to come, made his way to his bed.

The second tournament day started as bright as the first, the sun rising slowly over the tops of the distant mountains and turning the walls of the castle into a shining beacon on the hillside.

Merlin got up early, making his way through the already bustling servants' quarters and out of the castle, eager to try and get a head start with his duties on the tournament field. Watching the previous day's bouts had enthused him somewhat and he was keen to make a better impression on Arthur than he had yesterday. Arthur might be annoying and arrogant, but Merlin had come to respect his drive and professionalism in the arena, his skill with the sword, and he wasn't going to be the one to let the side down.

He opened the door to the armoury and stepped inside, looking in satisfaction at Arthur's armour and weapons hanging amongst those of his opponents. Merlin had done his best to ensure that everything had been properly cleaned and polished. By hand this time, mind you.

He was reaching for Arthur's helmet when a sudden

hiss made him look up. He cocked his head on one side, straining to hear. Had he imagined it? The armoury was silent. Shrugging, Merlin carried on gathering up the various pieces of Arthur's armour.

There was another hiss, low and angry sounding.

Merlin stopped, frowning. That *definitely* hadn't been his imagination. He peered into the gloomy corners of the armoury.

'Hello?'

He could see nothing but shadows and motes of dust drifting lazily in the rays of sunlight cast from the high windows. He made his way gingerly through the racks of carefully hung armour.

'Is someone there?'

He pushed aside one of the knights' cloaks and stopped suddenly at the sight of Valiant's striking yellow shield with its curling black snakes. For a fraction of a second, Merlin was convinced that one of the snakes was glaring at him with blazing red eyes. Just as quickly, the flare of red was gone, almost as if the creature had closed its eyelids.

Merlin crept forward to get a closer look at the shield. Whoever had painted the snakes had done a remarkable job. They were like no snake that Merlin could recognize – thick, horny spines jutting from their heads, the scales of their bodies bulging with knots of powerful muscle.

Tentatively Merlin reached out to touch the shield. As he did so, he felt a cold draft upon his back as someone opened the armoury door behind him. He turned slowly . . .

And found himself staring at the point of Knight Valiant's sword.

Chapter Six

'Can I help you with something, boy?' Valiant stared at Merlin suspiciously, his flashing grey eyes flicking down to the shield for a moment, a frown creasing his brow.

Merlin shook his head. 'Nope. I'm good. I was just . . . just gathering my master's armour.' Merlin jerked a thumb towards the bench where Arthur's armour lay in a neat pile.

Valiant moved the tip of the sword to Merlin's stomach, prodding him backwards.

'Then you'd better be on your way.'

'Right. No problem.'

Merlin hurried to back away, tripping and colliding with an elaborate suit of armour belonging to one of the eastern knights. There was a loud clatter and for a moment it looked as though the stand and all its contents was going to topple onto the floor. Merlin steadied it frantically, then with a last glance at Valiant, gathered up his own pile of armour and hurried out of the armoury door.

Valiant watched him go distrustfully, then knelt and inspected the shield carefully. The boy had been playing with fire. The snakes were always hungry first thing in the morning.

Smiling grimly, Valiant reached into his bag.

Merlin stood in Arthur's chambers watching with satisfaction as the prince inspected the gleaming suit of armour and crisply laundered tunic laid out on the table before him.

Arthur inspected each piece carefully, then looked over at Merlin in puzzled disbelief.

'You did all this on your own?'

'Yes, sire,' said Merlin proudly.

Arthur picked up the sword and examined the shining blade carefully. Merlin could tell that he was impressed. He suppressed the urge to smile. Arthur placed the sword back carefully on the table and turned to Merlin expectantly.

'Now let's see if you can get me into it without forgetting anything.'

Handling the armour by the edges so as to ensure

that he didn't smear the metal with his fingerprints, Merlin started work, checking that each piece was in its correct place before moving on to the next. He worked carefully and methodically, without rush or panic, ensuring that straps were tied tight enough to be secure, but not so tight that they restricted movement.

With the final piece of armour in place he stepped forward and presented Arthur with his sword. The prince took it, staring at Merlin in astonishment.

'That was much better.' He did his best to try and hide the surprise in his voice. 'Not that it could have got much worse.'

Merlin shrugged. 'I'm a fast learner.'

'I hope for your sake that's true.' Arthur snatched up his helmet and headed for the arena.

Merlin folded his arms in satisfaction. 'Good luck.'

Once again Arthur found himself surprised and confused by Merlin. After the previous day he had nearly decided to try and get into his armour unaided – anything to avoid Merlin's clumsy half-hearted bumbling. But the boy had obviously gone away and practised, learned from his mistakes. Arthur couldn't understand why. It had been obvious from the day they had met that the two of them had fairly low opinions of each other, but whereas most servants would just bite their lip and knuckle down, Merlin was constantly challenging him, constantly forcing him to re-evaluate himself and his opinions.

He should be finding it annoying, possibly even discourteous, but instead Arthur found Merlin's frank openness almost refreshing. He had been competing in the championships for many years now, and never once in that time had any of his servants ever wished him good luck, let alone one who wouldn't say it unless he really meant it.

It was surprising how much it heartened him.

Merlin followed Arthur out into the morning light, watching as the prince stepped out to the adulation of the crowd. Someone cheered his name and soon the entire audience was chanting and stamping their feet in rhythm. Despite himself Merlin found himself caught up in the moment, and before long he was clapping and cheering as loudly as the rest of them. He knew that he had done a good job this morning, and Arthur had known it too. Perhaps they were going to make a better team than either of them had thought.

'Is it my imagination, or are you beginning to enjoy yourself?' came a gruff voice.

Merlin turned to find Gaius standing beside him, a quizzical eyebrow raised.

Merlin grinned sheepishly. The truth was that, despite all the hard work, he *was* starting to enjoy himself. Not that he was prepared to admit that to Gaius, of course.

'It isn't totally horrible *all* of the time . . .'

Gaius just smiled, glad that Merlin was happy.

As the sun made its way across the brilliant blue of the sky, bout after bout unfolded in the arena below, each with its own unique blend of excitement, pageantry and danger. The crowds had cheered until they were practically hoarse, the fights Arthur and Valiant took part in bringing the loudest roars of astonishment and admiration.

Arthur had just competed in a spectacular fight with one of the eastern knights – a lithe, agile man who had danced across the arena in a riot of colour and whirling blades. It had taken all of Arthur's skill and expertise to win the bout, finally breaching the curved scimitars of his opponent with a series of dazzling feints and lunges that found their target with pinpoint accuracy.

The expectant crowd had gone wild as the royal emblem of Pendragon was moved up the scoreboard to the next round and an exhausted Arthur had staggered from the arena.

Merlin helped Arthur out of his armour, handing the prince a flagon of cold water. Arthur drank greedily. From the stands there was a roar of approval as Valiant entered the arena. Merlin and Arthur hurried over to watch. Valiant had to fight Sir Ewan, one of the knights of Camelot. Arthur's face was grim. Merlin knew that he was banking on Ewan being the first proper match for this arrogant knight from the Western Isles, but as the day had gone by it was becoming more difficult to discount the possibility that Valiant might make it through to the finals of this tournament.

The two combatants bowed low before Uther Pendragon and the applause of the people. Both knights were popular, but it was clear that Valiant was the crowd's favourite to win.

Merlin had met Sir Ewan several times during the tournament. He was well liked, quiet, and fiercely loyal to Camelot, his prince and his king. According to Arthur he was also a skilful and inventive swordsman. If there was anyone other than Arthur who could stop Valiant's remorseless progress then it was Sir Ewan.

Merlin's heart leaped in his chest as the two men clashed swords for the first time. The skills that he had witnessed in the arena over the last two days had given him a huge appreciation of the knights of Camelot, but skill alone might not be enough. Valiant was ruthlessly aggressive, wearing his opponents down with brute strength.

Sure enough, within moments he had Sir Ewan on the defensive as his sword smashed down again and again in huge, sweeping arcs, driving the young knight backwards.

The crowd roared their approval. Merlin saw Arthur's face cloud with anger and disappointment and Merlin grimaced. Creep or no creep, Valiant had certainly won the hearts of the audience. But his own meeting with Valiant in the armoury was still preying on his mind; Merlin had the sense that the knight was hiding something. Could it have something to do with how well he was doing in the tournament? Merlin shook his head. He was letting his imagination get the better of him. Valiant was just a strong swordsman, that was all.

A cheer brought his attention back to the arena. Perhaps incensed by the baying crowd, or perhaps finally confident that he had got the measure of his opponent, Ewan rallied back, spinning on his heels and unleashing a withering attack. Sparks flew as his sword blade connected with Valiant's vivid yellow shield.

Sensing a reversal of fortune the crowd started to urge Sir Ewan on.

Valiant sensed the crowd's change. He gave a snarl of anger. He had watched Ewan's bouts earlier in the day and had already made a mental note that the knight was going to be tricky to beat. He had hoped that by being aggressive in his initial attack he would be able to dispatch the young knight quickly, but Ewan had been more skilful in his defence than Valiant had expected and now, with the crowd rallying to his side, there was a danger that he would start to gain the upper hand.

Valiant swung his sword viciously, delivering blow after blow and driving Ewan back to the far side of the arena, away from the spectators. The savage attack took Ewan by surprise. His foot caught awkwardly in the dirt and he stumbled, crashing against the low arena wall, his helmet slipping from his head and clattering to the floor.

Seizing his opportunity, Valiant lunged, pinning Ewan to the ground with his shield.

'Strike him!' he hissed. 'Strike him!'

Ewan's eyes widened in horror as, unseen by the crowds, one of the snakes bulged out of the metal of Valiant's shield, eyes blazing with hatred.

Chapter Seven

Ewan struggled frantically to free himself as the snake bared long, wickedly sharp fangs, poison oozing from the tips. Before he could even draw breath to cry out, the snake's head snapped forward with terrifying speed, its jaws clamping down on Ewan's neck.

Within seconds, its deadly work done, the snake recoiled into the shield. Valiant raised his sword and brought it slamming down, completing the illusion that it was swordplay – not sorcery – that had felled his opponent, and turned triumphantly to the crowds.

There was a gasp of shock as Sir Ewan collapsed onto the floor. Valiant glanced across to where Morgana sat with her maidservant. She was staring at the crumpled body of Sir Ewan, a frown of concern creasing her beautiful features.

Valiant felt a surge of anger. This was his moment, his victory. The crowd should be applauding the success of the victor, not wasting their sympathy on the fate of the vanquished.

As Gaius, the court physician, hurried out into the arena, Valiant turned to where the steward was removing Sir Ewan's colours from the scoreboard and moving his own to the next tier. Valiant gave a nod of satisfaction. With or without the adulation of the crowd, he was one step closer to attaining his goal.

Merlin and Arthur watched as Gaius knelt down next to Ewan's fallen body. Merlin frowned as the physician called for help.

'I think he's badly hurt . . .'

Arthur watched with concern as four of the stewards bustled forward and lifted the young knight onto a stretcher. As the officials hurried from the arena with Gaius in tow, a mutter rippled through the crowd. Merlin wanted to say something, to reassure the prince that Gaius was a skilled doctor and that everything would be all right, but as the stretcher was carried past them Merlin caught Gaius' eye. The court physician looked worried. Very worried indeed.

★

Arthur had several more bouts to compete in that day, and night was already drawing in by the time Merlin had completed all his duties and returned to Gaius' chambers.

Ewan was stretched out on a bed on the far side of the room, Gaius sitting on a low stool by his side, dabbing at the knight's forehead with a damp cloth. Sir Ewan looked terrible, his sweat-soaked face a ghastly grey, his eyes sunk deep within his sockets and his hair hanging in lank strands across his scalp.

Merlin crossed to where Gaius sat.

'How is he?'

'It's most odd.' Gaius gestured for Merlin to come closer. 'Look at this.'

Gaius gently tipped Ewan's head to one side. Merlin leaned forward. There was a mark on the side of Ewan's neck; an angry red blotch and two tiny puncture marks.

'See these two small marks?' Gaius pointed. 'They look like a snake bite.'

'How can he have been bitten by a snake?' Merlin was puzzled. 'He was injured in a sword fight.'

'And yet his symptoms are consistent with poisoning. Slow pulse, fever, paralysis . . .'

'Can you heal him?' Merlin frowned.

Gaius slumped back in his chair with a sigh. 'If it is a snake bite,' he said, 'I need to extract venom from the snake that bit him to make an antidote.'

Merlin looked down at the pale, sweating figure on the bed. 'What happens if he doesn't get the antidote?'

Gaius' face was grim. 'Then I'm afraid there's nothing more I can do for him. He's going to die.'

'Maybe a snake got into the arena.' Merlin started to rack his brains. If they could only find it . . .

Before he could get too far down that particular train of thought, Gaius pointed out the flaw in his theory. 'How could a snake have bitten his neck whilst he was fighting?'

Merlin's face fell. Gaius was right. Then his brow creased as he suddenly remembered his encounter with Knight Valiant in the armoury that morning. The hiss that he had heard . . .

'He was fighting Knight Valiant,' he murmured.

'What was that?' Gaius was tending to Sir Ewan again.

'Nothing.'

Merlin turned and hurried out of the room.

Merlin made his way through the castle and out into the night air. Valiant was always the last knight to leave the field. He had refused the offer of a servant to help him with his armour, claiming that he had rituals and procedures of his own and that it would take too long to train someone new. Hopefully that would have meant that he hadn't got back to the castle yet, but Merlin wanted to make absolutely certain of that before he started poking around in his quarters.

He hurried across the courtyard and out through the castle gates. The arena was quiet and practically empty, the last few servants just finishing up in the preparation area, locking their masters' weapons in the armoury and gathering up armour and tunics to clean and repair. Merlin made a quick circuit of the field. He couldn't see Valiant anywhere. He cursed under his breath. He had left it too late. Valiant had obviously already finished and made his way back to his room. Merlin would have to wait for another opportunity.

He was just turning back towards the castle when a noise made him start. To one side of the castle gates, at the base of the wall, a dark figure caught his eye, slinking through the dark night. Merlin frowned. The figure was heading for the drainage moat that emerged from under the main entrance. What would anyone be doing sneaking around down there?

His curiosity aroused, Merlin hurried over to where

the figure had vanished into the shadows. Making his way cautiously down the slippery grass bank and keeping tight to the stone walls, he came to a heavy grille that covered the sewer mouth. It was open. Gagging at the stench, Merlin peered into the entrance of the narrow tunnel. He could hear the sounds of movement.

As he listened, there was the harsh tap of a flint being struck and light flared in the darkness as a torch was lit. Merlin jerked backwards, pressing himself hard against the wall as the flickering flame illuminated the mysterious figure. It was Valiant!

Heart hammering, Merlin waited for a few moments then peered into the tunnel mouth once more. Valiant was making his way deeper into the sewer. What on earth could he be doing?

Pulling his scarf up over his nose to mask the smell of stagnant water, Merlin started to creep down the tunnel, grimacing at the slippery silt that squelched beneath his feet. He moved slowly, aware that the slightest noise in the echoing passageway would give him away. Valiant had no such worries and the light from the torch became fainter and fainter as he made his way deeper into the bowels of the castle.

Abruptly the light vanished and Merlin had a moment of panic as the tunnel was plunged into total darkness.

He stopped, motionless in the blackness, waiting for his eyes to adjust. The pale moonlight filtering in from the sewer mouth was just enough to make out the vaguest of shapes. Merlin could see light glinting off the edge of a stone arch ahead of him. The tunnel must open out into a wider chamber. Faint sounds of movement drifted down the tunnel. He frowned. Whatever Valiant was doing, it had to be underhand for him to go to such extraordinary lengths to remain unseen. It had to have something to do with the encounter that they had had in the armoury. He had to find out what Valiant was doing!

Tiptoeing forward, Merlin made his way to the end of the tunnel and peered into the chamber beyond. It was a wide circular room, tunnels branching off in all directions to other parts of the castle. Merlin couldn't begin to imagine what a maze the lower sections of Camelot must be – it wasn't a place to get lost in.

In the centre of the chamber Valiant was crouched down, the torch resting on the floor by his side. He was fumbling with something. Merlin couldn't see what. There was a sudden scrabbling noise and a high-pitched terrified squeal. Valiant gave a grunt of satisfaction and straightened, scooping up the torch as he did so. Merlin ducked back behind the arch, suddenly realizing that if

Valiant came back out now then there was nowhere for him to hide.

Merlin stared at the flickering shadows cast across the wall by the torch, trying to work out the direction in which Valiant was moving. To his relief, the light moved away from the tunnel as Valiant crossed to the far side of the chamber. Grateful that whatever the task Valiant was engaged in, it was keeping him busy, Merlin hurried back down the tunnel towards the fresh air. It had been too dark in the sewers for him to see what Valiant was up to, but it was clearly something odd. He had a far better chance of working out what was going on if he could see properly.

Besides, Merlin was now convinced that Valiant was up to no good, and confronting the battle-skilled knight in a dark sewer with no chance of calling for help if the need arose was not the most ideal of conditions. Emerging into the open air, Merlin scrambled up the grass bank and tucked himself behind one of the statues that flanked the main gate. From here he could see the mouth of the tunnel and wait for Valiant to emerge.

He didn't have to wait long. Minutes later, Valiant emerged from the tunnel, checking that the coast was clear and locking the metal grille behind him. Merlin guessed that he must have stolen the key from somewhere. He held something in his left hand – something that looked like a small cage. Before Merlin had a chance to look more closely, Valiant tucked the object beneath his cloak and clambered up the slope towards Camelot once more.

Valiant swept in through the gates, his shield slung over his shoulder. Merlin followed, frowning. Why hadn't the knight left the shield in the armoury with the rest of his armour?

He followed Valiant at a safe distance, tailing him through the castle towards the quarters where all the visiting knights had been housed. Valiant unlocked the door to his chambers and vanished inside and Merlin scurried over to the door. Valiant had been impatient and the door hadn't latched shut properly. It was ajar.

Merlin peered through the crack. The room beyond looked empty, save for the shield resting on a wooden chair. There was no sign of Valiant. Merlin chewed his lip nervously. Did he dare try to sneak inside?

Before he could make up his mind about what he should do, Valiant stepped back into view, unlacing his cloak and placing the object that Merlin had seen down on the table in the middle of the room.

Merlin watched, puzzled. It *was* a cage. What on earth could Valiant want a cage for? He watched, fascinated, as Valiant opened the cage, reached inside for something and then straightened. To Merlin's surprise he was holding a mouse by its tail! Valiant must have been collecting mice from the sewer.

Holding the mouse firmly, Valiant leaned towards the shield. As if sensing its impending death, the mouse started to twist and struggle, squealing pitifully. 'Dinner time.' Valiant smiled unpleasantly.

Merlin watched in disbelief and horror as the surface of the shield started to ripple and twist and a low hissing sound filled the room. The struggling of the mouse became even more frantic. One by one the painted snakes bulged and swelled, then uncurled themselves from the surface of the shield, hissing with delight as they lunged at the dangling mouse. There was a snap of jaws as one of the snakes snatched out and the unfortunate rodent was swallowed whole.

Merlin gave a gasp of horror. Valiant was using sorcery! As he watched, Valiant reached for the cage again, the mice inside scrabbling desperately against the bars and the snakes hissing hungrily. Merlin's face was grim. He had to tell Gaius, and quickly. But as he turned to leave, his foot caught the edge of the door with a thump. The snakes' heads snapped round. Merlin's heart jumped as the blazing red eyes locked onto his.

They had heard him! They could see him!

He watched in terror as Valiant snatched up his sword and turned towards the door.

Chapter Eight

Valiant pulled open the door of his quarters suspiciously and looked out into the chamber beyond. He was certain he had heard something. More to the point, the snakes had heard something, and their hearing was considerably keener than his.

Hefting his sword in his hand, he stepped out of his room and looked around cautiously, his head cocked on one side, straining to hear anything that might reveal unwelcome visitors. The doors to the guests' quarters all led off a large square chamber, bare save for statuary and a fireplace. There was certainly nothing big enough for anyone to hide behind. He strode to the fireplace. No fire burned in the hearth, but there was also no way anyone could hide in the chimney without being seen. Crossing the chamber, he stepped out into the corridor that led back towards the main part of the castle. The stone passage was long and wide. Even if there had been someone spying on him, there was no way that anyone could have made it to the end of the passage in time.

Sword held out before him, he peered behind one of the pillars that lined the corridor, then stopped and gave a snort of disgust. He was being a fool. There was no one there. He was getting jumpy, that was all. Sheathing his sword, Valiant strode back to his chambers and slammed the door behind him.

As the door thumped shut, Merlin took a deep gasping breath and slipped out from behind a pillar a short way down the corridor. Perhaps having the build of a beanpole wasn't such a disadvantage after all. Still, if Valiant had decided to look behind *all* the pillars . . .

Merlin raced off, making his way through the castle, pushing past servants and courtiers. Angry voices called after him as he barged by a gaggle of servants busy preparing meals for the visiting knights. Merlin didn't have time to stop and apologize. He had to tell Gaius about what he had seen – it could be Sir Ewan's only hope.

He burst into the room, breathing heavily. Gaius looked up in alarm.

'What on earth—'

'It's Valiant. I was right . . .' gasped Merlin. He hurried over to where the old physician was tending to Sir Ewan. 'I saw the snakes.'

Ewan gave a moan, his head twisting in pain. Gaius caught Merlin by the arm and steered him away from the injured knight, sitting him down at the long wooden table and pouring him a glass of water.

'Here. Calm down, drink this and start at the beginning.'

Merlin drank gratefully, and then told Gaius of what he had seen in Valiant's chambers.

'I saw the snakes on Valiant's shield come alive. He's using magic.'

Gaius stared at him, his eyes clouded with concern. 'Are you sure?'

Merlin nodded. 'One snake ate a mouse, one gulp and it went straight down.' He looked over at the stricken knight lying pale and sweating on the other side of the room. 'Sir Ewan was fighting Valiant when he collapsed. It must have been one of the snakes from the shield that bit him.' Merlin got to his feet. 'I have to tell Arthur . . .'

Gaius caught his arm, worry creasing his brow. 'Is there any chance that you could have been mistaken?'

Merlin shook his head. 'I know magic when I see it.'

'Perhaps. But do you have any proof?'

Merlin stared at Gaius in disbelief. 'Don't you believe me?'

Gaius frowned. 'I fear that you're about to land yourself in trouble. How will you explain why you were in Valiant's chambers?'

'What does that matter?' pleaded Merlin. 'He's using magic to cheat in the tournament!'

'Maybe there's another explanation.'

Merlin couldn't believe this. Gaius was the one person that he had thought he could rely on to back him up. 'I saw it with my own eyes. Are you saying I'm lying?'

'No.' Gaius turned away. 'I don't know what you saw.' He turned back to Merlin, looking him full in the face. 'But you can't go accusing a knight of using magic without proof. The king will never accept the word of a servant over the word of a knight.'

Merlin glared at him angrily. 'So what I say doesn't count for anything . . . ?'

Gaius shook his head. 'I'm afraid it counts for very little as far as the king is concerned.' He dropped his eyes from Merlin's. 'That's just the way it is.'

Merlin watched as the old man shuffled back over to where Sir Ewan lay and started wiping his brow once more. He felt frustrated and hurt. Merlin had felt he could always rely on Gaius' advice, but now . . .

'Why don't you want me to do anything?' he pleaded.

'There's nothing you *can* do,' snapped Gaius. 'I don't want to hear another word about it.'

Fists clenched in frustration, Merlin crossed to his room, slamming the door behind him and throwing himself down onto the small bed.

Why wouldn't Gaius help him?

Despite all his special powers, he had never felt as lonely or helpless. What was the point of having the ability to do magic if he was unable to use that ability? The anger and pain that had been with him all his life surged within him, threatening to blot out everything else.

Gaius watched Merlin storm to his room with a heavy heart. He had not intended to hurt the boy. More than anything, he wanted to help him, and unfortunately that meant persuading him to keep quiet about what he had seen.

He had no doubt that what Merlin had told him was

the truth. Indeed, given Ewan's desperate condition, it was the only logical explanation. But he didn't think that Valiant was a sorcerer – if that was the case, then why would he go to all the trouble of fighting in the tournament? No, it was far more likely that he had been given the enchanted shield by another. Just enough power to conjure the snakes to do his will.

Gaius looked at the dying knight and shook his head angrily. If the king knew what one of his precious knights had done . . .

Gaius slumped onto a chair.

And there was the root of the problem. The king believed that the knights of the realm were upright, honourable men, beyond reproach from anyone, let alone a servant. If Merlin accused one of them without proof . . .

Gaius winced as he thought back to a tournament two summers ago when the sword of a visiting dignitary had been irreparably damaged. Suspicion had fallen on one of the servants, a young boy not much older than Merlin who had been responsible for stabling the dignitary's horse and ensuring that his belongings were taken to his rooms.

The poor lad had been completely innocent – the sword had actually been damaged by two of the visiting knights who had been in the stable and, impressed by the quality of the blade, had decided to test its metal against the wood of the stable door.

A badly placed nail had been the culprit that had done the damage, but when the young servant tried to convince Uther that it was the knights who were to blame, the king had flown into one of his terrible rages. To their shame, the two knights had stayed silent as the young lad had been locked into the stocks and left for nearly four days in the heat of the summer sun without food or water.

Both knights had been soundly beaten in the early stages of the tournament, and Gaius had taken great pleasure in suturing the wounds of one of them, so angry with him that he nearly didn't use any of his usual pain-dulling herbs for the operation. The young servant had left Camelot shortly after, vowing never to return.

Gaius gave a deep sigh. All Merlin needed to do was turn a blind eye for another day or so. Valiant would win the tournament, claim his prize and leave. It wasn't right, and it wasn't fair, but without unequivocal proof of Valiant's wrongdoing it was all they could do. In the meantime, he would use all of his ability to try and ease Ewan's pain and consult his books to see if there was anything that he could find to cure the young knight. It was a long shot he knew, but finding a non-magical solution would prevent Merlin from doing anything rash.

Merlin rose early the following day, purposely making his way down to the preparation area before Gaius was awake. It meant that he missed breakfast, but he didn't care. He was still angry and hurt that the old physician hadn't taken his claims seriously.

By the time Arthur arrived, Merlin had checked over his armour nearly a dozen times and was beginning to regret not having eaten. As he helped Arthur into his armour, he noted that the prince was staring over towards the far side of the preparation area. Merlin followed his gaze.

It was Sir Julius.

Merlin gulped. He had been so wrapped up in the dilemmas of what he should do about Valiant that he hadn't really taken much heed of the scoreboard, somehow missing the fact that Sir Julius had made it through to this stage of the tournament.

Not that it was much of a surprise; Sir Julius might not be the most skilful knight in the competition, but what he lacked in finesse, he made up for in sheer brute strength. He was nearly seven feet tall with a chest like one of the barrels from the cellar, and his servant was having to stand on a ladder just to get his armour tied on properly. Merlin couldn't imagine how heavy his enormous sword and shield had to be.

He turned back to Arthur and said nervously, 'You're telling me you have to fight him? But he's huge!'

'And as strong as a bear.' Arthur nodded thoughtfully. 'But he's slow.'

'And you're fast!'

'Exactly!'

Merlin handed Arthur his helmet, sword and shield and watched with admiration as his master headed out to face the giant Sir Julius.

Morgana gave a gasp as Julius and Arthur stepped forward to present themselves to Uther. Arthur's slim frame was dwarfed by the monster standing next to him.

'You're not worried, are you?' asked Gwen, amused.

Morgana realized that she was gripping her maidservant's arm a little too tightly. Embarrassed now, she let go.

'No.'

The two knights bowed before the king, then turned

to face each other. The crowd had none of their usual fervour and enthusiasm. The injury to Sir Ewan had cast a cloud over the proceedings, reminding them that this test of skill could also be a deadly game. They had no desire to see their prince cut down by this lumbering giant.

Julius launched his attack, but Arthur had been right – the man was big and heavy, and that meant that his armour was big and heavy too. He must have been carrying more than twice the weight of any of the other knights.

Every swing of that huge sword struck hard on the dirt floor of the arena, Arthur dancing out of the way with ease, then darting in close and landing blow after blow before Julius could raise the sword again.

Merlin watched in awe. Whatever he might have initially thought of Arthur as a person, he couldn't deny that he was a stupendous swordsman. The skill and precision that was being demonstrated in the arena spoke of someone who had trained and learned and honed his craft with dedication and determination. It made Merlin wonder if the brash, arrogant upstart whom he had first met really was the true Arthur or whether it was just a front.

As the bout went on, the crowd started to rally

behind their champion, and to ecstatic cheers Arthur finally landed the blow that sent Julius' massive bulk crashing to the ground.

Arthur was in the final.

With Julius defeated, Arthur's fights in the arena were over for the day. The bout had left him exhausted and he had retired to his chambers, leaving Merlin to get his armour ready for the final the following morning.

As Merlin worked, he kept a wary eye on Valiant who sat on the far side of the preparation area, getting ready for his next duel. Valiant picked up the shield and casually started to clean it. Merlin couldn't believe the nerve of the man.

'How are you getting on?' Merlin looked up to see Gaius standing over him.

'Fine,' snapped Merlin. 'I'm just doing my job, minding my own business.'

Gaius said nothing, his brow creasing with concern as he watched Valiant calmly polish his shield with its design of twisted snakes.

Merlin glanced over at the scoreboard. Valiant was only one fight away from the final. If he won his next bout . . .

Merlin and Gaius both watched anxiously as Valiant

got to his feet and entered the arena once more. Merlin watched carefully for any sign of Valiant using his shield, but the man was crafty – he obviously knew that to use the snakes was a risk, and that he only needed to use them when his adversary had a strong chance of beating him. At the moment Valiant had no such fears.

His opponent was the last of the eastern knights. The man was a clever and agile swordsman, but he was no match for Valiant. The fight was brutal and short. Valiant was viciously aggressive, dispatching his opponent with ruthless efficiency.

As he saluted the crowd in victory, the steward moved his colours to the final tier, placing them alongside the emblem of Pendragon.

Merlin turned to Gaius in despair.

'Valiant is going to fight Arthur in the final. He'll use the shield to kill him!'

Chapter Nine

That evening Merlin did none of his chores. How could he possibly polish and tend to Arthur's armour knowing that when he stepped out to meet Valiant in battle he was going to face certain death? The Great Dragon had told Merlin that it was his destiny to be Arthur's protector. At first Merlin had been certain that the Dragon had to be wrong – about one of them at any rate. Merlin had thought Arthur to be petty and childish, a boy abusing his position of power, but the last few days had given him a different impression of the young prince – a glimpse of the man who was waiting inside the boy. Surely now, with that knowledge, he should be doing something to protect him?

Instead, he sat in the gloom of the physician's chambers, listening to the ragged, troubled breathing of Sir Ewan, frustrated and angry at his inability to come up with a solution. He was a sorcerer, for heaven's sake, and a powerful one at that if Gaius was right about him, but to use magic to unmask what Valiant was doing would condemn him to a death far quicker than that offered by a snakebite.

No. The only way that he was going to be able to expose Valiant's treachery was to let Uther and the others see it for themselves. But how? The sun was going to rise in less than twelve hours and then there would be no chance to do anything before Arthur had to face him in the arena.

The door on the far side of the room swung open and Gaius entered, crossing to Sir Ewan's side to check on his fever. Merlin didn't look up.

'Merlin.' Gaius' voice broke the awkward silence. 'About what I said yesterday. Uther wouldn't listen to you or me, but it's not that I don't believe you . . .' The old physician paused. Merlin waited. 'Sometimes it's hard to know what to say . . .' Gaius sounded weary. 'I don't have all the answers.' He sighed. 'What I'm trying to say is . . . you're right. We can't let Valiant get away with this.'

Merlin felt a rush of relief. At last he had an ally again. He had known in his heart that Gaius was only doing his best to protect him, and he knew that what

Gaius had said was right – the king was never going to accept the accusations of a servant.

'But we don't have proof.' Merlin looked up at the old man unhappily, repeating the same argument that Gaius had used yesterday.

Gaius pursed his lips thoughtfully. 'If we could cure Ewan, he can tell the king that Valiant is using magic. The king will believe another knight.'

Merlin could have kicked himself. Of course. It was so simple. Gaius had said it himself on the day that Ewan had been injured. They needed to get hold of the snake that had bitten him.

Gaius was shaking his head. 'How we get the antidote, well, that's another matter . . .'

But before Gaius had even finished his sentence, Merlin had gone.

Merlin hurried through the castle towards the royal chambers. The king had summoned all the knights in Camelot to dine with him to toast the two successful finalists. That meant Valiant had to be there. If Merlin could be sure that he was going to be away from his chambers, even for a short time . . .

As he scurried through the servants' quarters, he snatched up one of the aprons of the king's servants from a pile of dirty laundry. He needed to be absolutely certain that Valiant was at the feast. It was unlikely that the knight would do anything to anger the king, but having watched the way Valiant worked Merlin wouldn't put it past him to make some plausible excuse to leave the banquet to further his own plans if he had to. Unfortunately, Arthur would definitely be there, and if Merlin was spotted by him then there were bound to be some awkward questions asked.

Merlin scampered up a winding staircase and into a room bustling with cooks preparing a meal for the assembled knights. He slipped into a line of servants all waiting to be given something to take to the king's chambers. No one gave him more than a second glance; they were all working furiously to ensure that nothing kept the king and his guests waiting.

A plate of cold meats was thrust into Merlin's hands and he was shooed away impatiently. Taking a deep breath and praying that Arthur wasn't in a seat which faced the door, Merlin slipped into the king's quarters.

Uther and the knights were sitting at a vast oak table in the centre of the room. To Merlin's relief, Arthur was seated on the king's right, facing away from the door. Valiant was there too, on the other side of the king, but he was far too intent on making a good impression on Uther to notice a mere servant.

Merlin was ushered quietly to one side and the plate he was carrying was whipped from his hand by one of the king's aides. Merlin stepped back into the shadows of the room, watching and listening carefully.

Uther took a long drink of ale from a foaming flagon. 'So, Valiant, do you think you have a chance of defeating my son?'

A sly smile curled at the edges of Valiant's mouth. 'He is a great warrior, my lord. I hope to prove myself a worthy opponent.'

Merlin grimaced. Could the guy be any slimier? Uther, however, seemed totally taken in by Valiant's apparently chivalrous nature.

'You should stay in Camelot after the tournament,' Uther said. 'I could use more knights like you.'

'I'd be honoured, my lord.' Valiant gave a bow of his head then glanced across at Arthur. Merlin couldn't see the prince's face, but he could tell by the way that his back stiffened that he wasn't pleased.

The king called for more ale, and servants hurried forward in their dozens. Merlin had seen all that he needed to. Valiant was going to be in the king's company for a little while yet. That should give him all the time he needed.

Using the bustle of bodies as cover, he slipped out of the room.

Merlin hurried to the guests' quarters, discarding his borrowed apron as he ran. Valiant might be distracted for the moment, but with the tournament final the following day, it was unlikely that he would stay long in the king's company. Besides, Merlin had no wish to spend any more time with that enchanted shield than was absolutely necessary.

He crept towards Valiant's chambers and pulled at the door. Locked. Hardly surprising. Checking that no one was watching, Merlin stretched out his hand and muttered a single harsh word under his breath.

'*Allinan.*'

A flare of heat rose within his body, and for a moment the outer chamber was lit up as Merlin's eyes flashed with a glittering, golden glow.

There was a click as the door unlocked. The glow faded from Merlin's eyes as he gingerly pushed the door ajar and slipped inside.

The room was gloomy and cold, the light from the moon in the night sky outside the tall, narrow window casting long shadows across the floor. A huge fireplace dominated one wall, but glowing embers in the hearth were all that remained of the fire. Merlin shivered. In the centre of the room the shield sat propped up on a high-backed chair. On the table alongside it sat the small wooden cage that Valiant had used to trap the mice from the sewer. Merlin crossed to the table and peered inside. It was empty. Obviously the snakes had healthy appetites.

Cautiously Merlin approached the shield. In the cold moonlight it didn't look like anything special – just an ordinary metal shield with a grotesque design painted on the front. There was no sign of the glowing eyes that Merlin had caught sight of the other day, no sign that the surface of the metal had come to horrible, writhing life, no hint that the snakes were anything more than paint. It was no wonder that Gaius had done his best to dissuade him from going to Arthur with his story. Without proof it would seem like the ravings of a madman.

Merlin suddenly realized that he had no idea how he was going to entice the snakes to manifest themselves. He had set out with the grand idea of capturing one of them so that Gaius could manufacture his antidote, but he had no idea how he was actually going to go about it.

He looked around the room. Perhaps Valiant had some book or potion that he used. He shook his head. No. That was a stupid idea. Valiant needed to be sure that he could enchant the snakes in the arena at a moment's notice, and that meant that it had to be a word or phrase.

He hadn't been aware of any spell being uttered when he had witnessed the snakes being fed, but perhaps if they were hungry they had the ability to bring themselves to life when food was offered. With a distinct shortage of mice, Merlin briefly considered offering his arm to the shield in order to tempt the snakes out, but then remembered how swiftly Sir Ewan had succumbed to their venom and quickly thought better of it.

Next to the table was a wooden rack with Valiant's sword resting in it. Merlin took the sword and hefted it in his hand. Standing a good distance back from the shield, he poked at one of the coiling snakes with the tip of the sword. There was nothing but the hard tap of metal on metal.

Merlin frowned. How was he going to bring the snakes to life?

A noise from the corridor made him spin – footfalls on flagstones. Merlin stared across at the door in horror.

Surely Valiant couldn't have left the banqueting room already? He looked around the room frantically. Even if he could find a suitable place to hide, there was no way that he would be able to get the sword back into its rack in time. As the footsteps came closer and closer, Merlin closed his eyes and desperately tried to remember some of the spells that he had read about in the book that Gaius had given him. Was there some way he could use magic to prevent discovery?

The footsteps stopped outside the door. It was too late!

Behind Merlin, unseen, a pinpoint of red light flickered in the eyes of one of the snakes. Tongue flicking from between its needle-sharp teeth, the snake writhed and twisted, its scaly body bulging into obscene life as it curled from the painted surface of the shield.

In stealthy silence it slid down the leg of the chair and started to slither across the stone floor towards the young warlock. Sensing warmth in the cold dark of the room, it reared up, fangs bared, ready to strike at its prey.

Chapter Ten

At the sound of a key being rattled in a lock, Merlin thought that it was all over, but then he realized with sudden relief that the key was being used in the room next door! The sounds in the corridor weren't Valiant at all, but another knight returning to his quarters.

Merlin let out his pent-up breath in a rush. Days like these were going to take years off his life! He let his head drop, taking in a deep lungful of air.

And suddenly noticed a shadow cast by the moon.

He stared in horror as the long, sinuous shadow, quivering with tension, arched itself into a tight curve. Merlin didn't even stop to think what he was doing. He span, lashing out with Valiant's sword, feeling the blade slice though flesh and muscle and bone with a sickening jolt. The snake gave a horrible bubbling scream as its head was severed from its body and sent bouncing across the room. The body curled and thrashed, thick black blood spraying from its neck and splattering over the floor.

Sensing the death of their fellow, the two remaining snakes burst from the shield, spitting and hissing with anger. The muscular body of one of them dropped to the floor with a heavy thud as it pulled itself completely free of the shield. The other coiled up onto the back of the chair glaring at Merlin with malevolent red eyes.

Despite his terror, Merlin had come too far to leave without the proof that he desperately needed. Warding off the lunging snakes with the sword, he edged past the oozing corpse of the one that he had killed, reached out and grabbed the severed head that lay in a pool of blood by the fireplace.

The snakes darted forward, almost as if they were trying to stop him. Merlin slashed wildly at them as they slithered lightning-quick across the smooth stone floor. He scooped up the head with his free hand, grimacing as the thick blood leaked into his palm.

Knowing that there was no point in trying to conceal his break-in any more, Merlin hurled the sword at the snapping snakes and threw himself towards the door, the severed head clutched tightly to his chest.

He hared down the corridor, his heart pounding. He

had done it! Once Gaius had made the antidote, Valiant would be finished. He had fulfilled his destiny, he had saved Arthur! Merlin felt a rush of pride. Not only had he saved the prince, but he had ensured that the tournament would be won fairly and honourably. Perhaps some of Arthur's training was beginning to rub off on him . . .

Valiant knew that something was wrong as soon as he heard the echo of running feet down the long stone corridor. He turned the corner just in time to catch a glimpse of a fleeing figure heading back towards the main part of the castle. The door to his chamber was open.

He cursed under his breath. No prize for guessing who the culprit was: Arthur's busybody of a servant. One look at the chaos inside was enough for him to piece together what had happened. The body of the dead snake lay in a pool of thick, black blood and the two surviving reptiles lurked in the shadows in the corner of the room, red eyes blazing.

Valiant closed the door and bolted it. He should have taken more heed of Arthur's nosy servant when he'd caught him snooping around the armoury. The boy had obviously seen the snakes, and had now seen enough to alert him to the fact that the shield was not all that it appeared to be. He would almost certainly tell Arthur and the king what he had seen. Not a problem in itself – Valiant was certain that the king would side with a knight of the realm if it came to a simple matter of word against word – but if the boy had proof . . .

Valiant stooped and picked up the body of the dead snake. Blood dripped from its severed neck onto the floor. He glanced across to where another smaller pool of blood stained the floor near the fireplace. The head. The boy had taken the head.

Valiant sat down heavily. He had to think quickly. From the day that he had heard of Devlin the sorcerer and the shield that he possessed, from the moment that he had hatched his plan in a dark tavern on the edge of the Forest of Balor, he had always known that what he intended was going to be dangerous. Cheating at the royal tournament of Uther Pendragon was bad enough; using sorcery to cheat and getting caught was a sure way of securing an unpleasant death. He glanced at the snake's headless body. That would be his fate, too, if Uther believed the boy.

Valiant stood up and crossed to the fireplace, piling more logs into the grate and kneeling down to blow on the glowing embers, coaxing them into roaring life once more. As soon as the flames had caught on the dry timber, he tossed the body of the snake onto the fire, then turned to where the other snakes lurked in the shadows.

'Back to where you came from! Until I need you again.'

He pointed at the shield. Hissing angrily, the snakes glided across the floor, winding up the leg of the chair and melting back into the surface of the metal once more.

Valiant undid his cloak and tossed it onto the bed. Snatching up a blanket, he tore off a strip and knelt on the floor, wiping at the congealing pool of blood that glistened on the flagstones. When all trace of the blood had gone, he threw the blanket onto the fire as well and sat back heavily in one of the high-backed chairs, watching as the flames consumed all evidence of the snake's existence.

Let the boy try and accuse him now. Head or no head, there was no way that the servant would ever convince the king that a knight had used sorcery. It wasn't chivalrous or noble enough. Valiant snorted. The king was a foolish old man with outdated ideas. A knight should use all means at his disposal to defeat an enemy, and if that meant using witchcraft then Valiant was all for it. It had got him to the final, it would get him his prize, and it would get him the Lady Morgana.

All those who had it in them to stop him were disgraced or dying. A frown flickered across Valiant's face as he remembered Sir Ewan. The knight had been strong; the bite he had received hadn't finished him off as quickly as Valiant had expected. If the boy had the head, then the old physician, Gaius, might well be able to make an antidote.

Valiant sat forward in his chair, staring into the flames that roared in the hearth, thinking frantically. If the accusation was made against him by another *knight*, then the king would be far more likely to take it seriously. He rubbed at his jaw. He would have to ensure that Sir Ewan died before any antidote could take effect. Smiling to himself, Valiant turned to the shield once more . . .

Gaius examined the head of the snake with distaste. He had been right in his suspicions. It was a species of snake found in the Forest of Balor – nasty, vicious creatures with an affinity to the old magic. The unpleasant effects of their venom made them popular with those who practised the dark arts, and the snakes' speed and aggression made it practically impossible to capture them to make antidotes.

He snatched up a large jar from the table, hooking

the snake's wickedly sharp fangs over the lip and squeezing the venom sacs on either side of its head. A thick, milky liquid oozed from the tips of the teeth and pooled in the bottom of the jar.

Gaius nodded in satisfaction. 'I'll get started on preparing an antidote.'

'I'm going to tell Arthur,' said Merlin.

'You'll need this.' Gaius handed him the snake's head.

Merlin took it and turned towards the door.

'Merlin.'

As Merlin looked back over his shoulder, Gaius smiled at him proudly.

'What you did. It was very brave.'

Merlin smiled back at him, and hurried off to find Arthur.

Arthur listened as Merlin told him about everything that he'd seen since his encounter with Valiant in the armoury. Arthur barely paid it any attention, the story was so fantastic. He busied himself with one of his swords.

'Valiant is using a magic shield!' cried Merlin, desperate to be heard.

His servant sounded so earnest, so serious, that Arthur

111

suddenly felt compelled to listen to what he had to say more carefully. He put down the sword.

'A magic shield?'

'The snakes on it come alive,' explained Merlin breathlessly. 'I chopped off one of their heads . . .' He pointed at the severed head that lay on Arthur's table.

Arthur picked up the head and examined it. It was an ugly-looking brute. He looked at Merlin dubiously.

'You? You chopped its head off?'

'Sir Ewan was bitten by a snake from the shield when he was fighting Valiant.' Merlin was desperate to convince him. 'Talk to Gaius! You can see the puncture marks on Sir Ewan's neck where the snake bit him!'

Arthur frowned. It was true that Ewan losing the fight had taken him by surprise, but to defy the laws of the land so blatantly, to use such underhand means . . . He shook his head.

'Valiant wouldn't dare use magic in Camelot.'

'Sir Ewan was pinned behind Valiant's shield. No one could see the snake bite him.' Merlin sounded so certain.

Arthur put the snake's head back down on the table. Valiant might be a little crude in his fighting style, and he was cocky, but he was still a knight.

'I don't like the guy, but that doesn't mean he's cheating.'

'Gaius is preparing an antidote to the snake venom,' said Merlin confidently. 'When Sir Ewan's conscious he'll tell you what happened.'

Arthur frowned. Ewan was a trusted knight of Camelot. If he confirmed Merlin's story . . .

'If you fight Valiant in the final, he'll use the shield. It's the only way he can beat you!' Merlin snatched up the head and thrust it at Arthur. 'Look at it! Have you ever seen any snakes like this in Camelot?'

Arthur stared at the head. It was true. This was no ordinary snake. And Merlin had to have got it from somewhere.

Merlin took a deep breath. 'I know I'm just a servant. My word doesn't count for anything. But I wouldn't lie to you.'

Arthur looked at him curiously. There was such sincerity in his voice, such desperation in his eyes.

'I want you to swear to me that what you're telling me is true.' Arthur watched his servant's face for any sign that this was some trick, some deception.

Merlin met his gaze. 'I swear it's true.'

Arthur stared at his servant for a moment, then nodded. 'Then I believe you.'

Merlin gave a gasp of pride and relief.

The two stared at each other, Arthur suddenly aware of how much he had come to trust his new servant. Merlin had revealed himself to be far more than Arthur had first thought. He had proved himself loyal and hard-working, he had earned a certain amount of respect, and that growing respect seemed to be mutual. It seemed ludicrous that he would throw all that away on some flight of fancy. They had both had their suspicions about Valiant from the beginning; now it seemed that those suspicions were well founded

'Then what do we do now?' Merlin asked.

'The king must know, said Arthur. 'The tournament must be postponed until Valiant has explained himself.'

'He's going to try and wriggle out of it.' Merlin looked nervous at the thought of having to take his accusations before the king. Arthur didn't blame him. His father was fastidious when it came to rules and regulations, particularly when it came to matters of honour. They would have to do everything by the book.

'I know.' Arthur nodded. 'You go and wake the tournament officials. Tell them that all fights are to be delayed until after the court has met.'

Merlin nodded. 'What are you going to do?'

'Wake the chief councillor,' said Arthur. 'And tell him to summon the king.'

High above them, unseen in the rafters that crisscrossed the ceiling of Arthur's chambers, a dark, sinuous shape wound its way stealthily through the shadows, red eyes glinting in the candlelight.

The snake had been given a task by its master. It would not fail.

Chapter Eleven

When the guards came for him, Valiant put up no resistance, made no protestation. His part in the proceedings would play out once he was in front of the king and not before.

The guards directed him to pick up his shield and walk ahead of them. Servants watched in alarm as Valiant was escorted out of the guests' quarters and across the great courtyard of Camelot.

The throne room was already abuzz with officials and courtiers woken from their slumber, confused as to why the court had been summoned and the day's entertainment in the arena postponed. A murmur rippled through the room as Valiant was ushered in by the guards.

Valiant could see Arthur and his servant watching expectantly as he entered. A smile played at the corners of his lips as the guards marched him before the throne. Elsewhere in the castle one of his snakes was poised to strike. Arthur and his young servant were going to get a surprise when they called for their witness . . .

A flicker of concern ran through Merlin as Valiant was shepherded forward. He wasn't acting like a man on the defensive. On the contrary, he looked more confident and cocksure than ever. Arthur sensed it, too, and shot Merlin a worried glance.

Before either of them had a chance to work out what Valiant was plotting, a nervous hush fell over the throne room and Uther Pendragon, his face clouded with anger, swept into the room like a storm.

Merlin, Arthur and the members of the royal court all watched with uneasy expectation as the king took his seat on the throne of Camelot. An advisor hurried to his side, whispering animatedly and gesturing towards Arthur. Merlin took a deep breath. He suddenly realized what a huge responsibility Arthur had taken upon himself in summoning the court. He was a prince of the realm and as such was expected to follow the law to the letter. If Uther didn't believe them now, then the prince could be finished in the eyes of his people. Merlin gulped. They would both be finished.

The advisor stepped away from the throne and Uther stared in anger at his son.

'Why did you summon the court?'

Arthur stepped forward. 'I believe that Knight Valiant is using a magic shield to cheat in the tournament.'

The court erupted.

Gaius had worked all night on the antidote. The snake had only provided a very small amount of venom for him to work with, but he still needed to conduct tests to ensure that he had the right mixture before giving it to Ewan. Giving him the wrong antidote would kill him just as surely as doing nothing at all.

Curing Ewan was now of paramount importance. Now that Merlin had taken his story to Arthur, there was no question that this would go before the king, and without Sir Ewan's testimony Merlin's story would never be believed.

Where Valiant had used the castle mice as food, Gaius used them as test subjects, poisoning them with tiny quantities of venom and then administering various versions of the antidote. The line of dead mice lying on the table were testament to how complex the snake's venom was – and how difficult the antidote was to prepare.

Gaius stretched, wincing as his back cracked alarmingly. Dawn light was filtering through the windows. By now the court would have gathered, accusations would have been made and questions would be being asked. He could wait no longer.

He peered at where two mice scurried happily around in their cage. He had given them both the latest batch of antidote over an hour ago and the results had been quite encouraging. Since then they had shown no ill effects from their ordeal. Now it was time to see if the antidote worked equally well on humans.

He picked up a small phial from the table. If he had done his job correctly then the few small drops of clear liquid that glistened in the bottom of the jar would revive Sir Ewan. If not, then he feared that the young man had less than an hour to live.

'So you've got nothing to lose, have you?' murmured Gaius to himself.

He crossed to where the young knight lay on the low bed. Sir Ewan barely looked alive; his face was pale and streaked with sweat, his breathing hardly perceptible. Gaius pulled a stool to the side of the bed, sitting down next to Ewan and gently raising his head. Carefully he tipped the phial, letting tiny droplets of the clear liquid drip between the knight's dry, cracked lips.

Ewan swallowed as the antidote trickled into his mouth, coughing as the bitter taste caught at the back of his throat. Suddenly he stiffened, his face creasing with pain, his hands clenching at the sweat-soaked blankets. With a gasp he collapsed back onto the bed, silent and still. For one horrible second, Gaius thought that he had left it too late, but then Ewan took a deep, shuddering breath and his chest started to rise and fall with strong, steady breaths. His eyelids flickered open.

Gaius smiled with relief. 'Welcome back.'

Ewan stared up at him woozily, looking around in confusion as he struggled to work out where he was and what had happened to him.

'Gaius?'

'You're quite safe,' said Gaius, gently patting his arm. 'You're in my chambers. You're a very lucky young man.'

Ewan licked at his parched lips. 'Do you have any water?'

'Of course.'

Gaius crossed to the table, filled a tankard with water and gave it to Ewan. The knight drank greedily, water splashing over his chin. He coughed.

'Not so fast.' Gaius took the cup from him. 'Do you

recall anything of what happened? Do you remember your fight in the arena?'

Ewan thought for a moment, his brow creasing as he tried to sort through his jumbled memories. 'I remember how strong Valiant was, how determined. I thought that I had found the measure of him but then . . .'

Ewan's eyes widened in horror as the memory of the final moments of his battle with Valiant returned to him.

'There was a snake on his shield! It came alive!'

He struggled to rise from his bed, but Gaius gently pushed him back down. 'You're weak. The snake's venom is still in your system.'

'I must warn Arthur!'

'Arthur already knows,' Gaius said calmly. 'He's requested an audience with the king.'

Ewan relaxed slightly. Gaius patted his arm. 'I'll prepare a potion of fresh herbs to give you the strength to testify. Rest a moment. I won't be long.'

Gaius got to his feet and crossed to one of the tall cupboards that lined the walls. He peered at the rows of glass bottles and bags that lined the shelves. With a curse he realized that most of the herbs that he needed were in the bag that he had taken to the arena the day before – and left there.

He remembered that the palace cook had gathered a mound of fresh herbs ready for the feast after the tournament. A few handfuls would be quite sufficient for Sir Ewan's needs and the cook owed him a favour after Gaius had healed a nasty burn that he'd got from a cauldron of soup the week before.

Aware that every moment was vital, Gaius hurried out of the room.

From the rafters of the physician's chambers, spiteful red eyes watched the old man leave before turning their attention towards the knight on the bed.

The snake had been curled in the shadows for hours, watching, waiting for an opportunity to strike at its target, but the old man hadn't ever left the room, and the snake hadn't been given a single moment when it could complete its task.

'Finish the job you were designed for,' it had been told by its master. 'Finish the job you started in the arena, but on no account allow yourself to be seen by anyone other than your victim.'

With its prey finally alone and helpless, the snake seized its opportunity. Uncoiling itself from its hiding place, it slid down through the books and shelves that covered the walls, keeping to the shadows, moving quickly and quietly towards the prone knight.

It hesitated at the table where the old man had worked, torn between its desire to feed on the two mice that scurried agitatedly in their cage and completing the task that its master had commanded of it.

In this instance, obedience took precedence over instinct and the snake continued downwards. When it reached the floor, it surged onwards like a shaft of black lightning. Aware that something was in the room with him, the man on the bed tried to raise himself. The snake darted forward, slipping silently under the blankets. Suddenly Sir Ewan cried out as the snake wound its coils around his body, pinning his arms to his sides. He struggled helplessly as the snake's head emerged from beneath the blankets and hovered inches from his own, staring into his eyes.

The snake's forked tongue flicked out, tasting the knight's fear. It bared its fangs.

And struck.

Merlin watched with uneasy expectation as Uther Pendragon took in the accusation made by his son. Whispers rippled through the assembled courtiers; they all knew what the allegations would mean if they were true. Uther's face darkened dangerously and the murmers faded to silence. Uther turned to where Valiant stood flanked by guards.

'What do you have to say about this, Valiant?'

Valiant shook himself free of the guards and stepped forward, head held high and proud. 'My lord, this is ridiculous. I have never used magic.' He kept his voice low and calm, always respectful. He stared at Arthur defiantly. 'Does your son have any evidence to support this outrageous accusation?'

Uther glared at Arthur, giving no doubt as to his displeasure.

'Do you have any evidence?' he snapped.

'I do.'

Merlin hurried forward to the prince's side, holding out the head of the dead snake. Uther stared at it in bemusement. Merlin held his breath.

This was the moment of truth . . .

Gaius pushed open the door to his chambers and bustled inside, bunches of herbs in his arms. He dumped them down on the table and reached for a book on medicinal remedies.

He flicked through the book, grimacing as he read the instructions about how to prepare the medication.

'I'm afraid that this potion will taste like toad water, but it will get you back on your feet . . .'

Gaius stopped, staring in shock at Sir Ewan. The knight was sprawled half in and half out of the bed, his head resting at an awkward angle on the cold stone floor. Gaius hurried forward, but he already knew from the expression on the young man's face that there was nothing he could do.

For a moment he feared that it had been his antidote that had killed Sir Ewan, some mistake in the preparation that had caused a delayed reaction, but as he knelt down and saw the fang marks in Ewan's neck and chest, he knew that this had been no unfortunate accident.

He closed the dead knight's eyes, his face grim. By now Arthur and Merlin would have confronted Valiant, but the man was one step ahead of them. Merlin had been right. The man was dangerous, a killer. Looking warily around for any evidence that the snake was still at large, Gaius clambered to his feet and backed out of the room. He had to get to the throne room! He hurried off, knowing in his heart that it was already too late. By now Arthur and Merlin would have taken their suspicions to the king – and with their only witness dead, they had no way to substantiate their claims.

Chapter Twelve

Arthur watched nervously as Uther inspected the severed snake's head. He handed it back to Merlin and turned to Valiant.

'Let me see this shield,' snapped the king.

Valiant stepped forward, the shield held before him.

'Don't let him get too close,' whispered Merlin in alarm. Valiant wasn't stupid enough to kill the king in front of the entire royal household, but there was no way of telling how much control he truly had over the black snakes.

'Be careful, my lord.' Arthur drew his sword. 'The snakes from the shield come alive and even when they do their image remains on the shield.'

Uther frowned, clearly not believing a word of it. Ignoring Arthur's protestations, he reached out and

tapped the shield with his knuckles. Nothing happened.
No red eyes, no hiss, no coiling snakes. Arthur could see
a smile flicking across Valiant's face.

To his relief he saw Gaius enter the room. The old
physician beckoned frantically to Merlin.

Arthur was worried at the expression on the old
man's face. 'Where's Ewan?' he hissed desperately to
Merlin. 'Find out what's happening.'

Merlin hurried over to Gaius. Valiant was now
showing Uther the back of the shield.

'As you can see, my lord, it's just an ordinary
shield . . .'

Uther took the shield, testing its weight. Arthur
could already sense the mood of the court was changing;
the king could see no evidence of foul play and Valiant
was playing the part of the maligned and unjustly treated
victim perfectly. Arthur was beginning to look like a
fool and a liar.

'He's not going to let everyone see the snakes come
alive,' Arthur said desperately.

Uther looked at him with anguish. 'Then how am I
to know that what you say is true?'

'I have a witness,' said Arthur defiantly. 'Knight
Ewan was bitten by one of the snakes from the shield.
The venom made him grievously ill, but he has received

an antidote. He'll confirm that Valiant is using magic.'

A frown crossed Uther's face. Arthur knew that he held Sir Ewan in high regard. The two men had ridden together on many hunts and Uther had been very complimentary about Ewan's performance in the tournament. Arthur watched Valiant's response carefully. Surely this revelation would wipe that smug smile from his face. To his despair, Arthur saw nothing but triumph in Valiant's eyes.

'Where is this witness?' asked Uther impatiently.

'He should be here . . .' Arthur turned to where Merlin and Gaius were arguing in the doorway. Merlin looked terrified. Arthur felt a jolt of panic. Something was wrong.

'What is this?' snapped the king.

Merlin hurried back to Arthur's side, looking terribly worried.

'Where's Ewan?' Arthur whispered desperately.

'He's dead.' Merlin's voice was grave.

'Dead?' Arthur couldn't believe it. 'But the antidote . . .'

Merlin shook his head.

Arthur closed his eyes in disbelief. Their one chance of exposing Valiant had gone. Either by luck or by his own design, the man had outwitted them. Already he could hear the wagging tongues of the court, feel the gaze of everyone on him, waiting to hear what he had to say now. He turned slowly to face his father once more.

'I'm afraid the witness is dead.'

'So you have no proof of these allegations.' The king's voice was trembling with anger. 'Have you seen Valiant using magic?'

'No,' Arthur shook his head. 'But my servant—'

'Your servant!' Uther spat the word. 'You make these wild accusations against a *knight* on the word of your servant?'

'I believe he's telling the truth!' cried Arthur.

For a moment Arthur thought that his father was going to strike him – he had never seen him so incensed. The court held its breath as father and son faced each other.

'My lord,' Valiant stepped forward, a picture of quiet, calm dignity. Arthur had never hated anyone more. 'Am I really to be judged on the hearsay from a servant?'

'I'm not lying!' Merlin pushed forward angrily. 'I've seen the snakes come alive!'

Arthur groaned. Speaking up against Valiant was possibly the worst thing that Merlin could have done at that moment.

VALIANT

'How dare you interrupt!' Uther exploded with rage. 'Guards! Take him to the dungeons.'

The guards who had been on either side of Valiant rushed forward, grasping Merlin by the arms and dragging him towards the door.

'My lord.' Valiant's voice was like silk and he smiled smugly at Merlin. 'I'm sure he was merely mistaken. I would not want him punished on my account.'

Uther gestured to the guards to stop. 'See.' Uther glared at Arthur with anger and disappointment. 'This is how a knight behaves. With gallantry and honour.'

Arthur let his head drop. Nothing he could say would convince his father of Valiant's guilt now. He had failed. Valiant had won.

But the knight had not finished

'My lord.' Valiant leaned close to the king, but spoke loud enough for the whole court to hear. 'If your son made these accusations because he's afraid to fight me, then I'll graciously accept his withdrawal.'

Arthur felt himself flush with embarrassment. He could see the shame on his father's face.

'Is this true?' Uther's voice was low. 'Do you wish to withdraw from the tournament?'

'No!'

'So what am I supposed to make of these allegations?'
Uther's voice was full of pain and anger.

Arthur knew that he had only one course open to
him. In the eyes of his father, in the eyes of the court,
he was a liar – Valiant had made sure of that. He wasn't
going to let them think him a coward as well. And he
wasn't going to give Valiant the satisfaction of winning
the tournament without having to face him in battle. At
least in the arena he could prove his worth to his
father.

'There's obviously been a misunderstanding.' Arthur
straightened, mustering as much dignity as he could. 'I
withdraw the accusation against Knight Valiant.' He
turned to the knight. 'Please accept my apologies.' He
could barely bring himself to utter the words.

Valiant inclined his head. 'Accepted.'

Bowing to the king, Arthur turned to leave. The
entire court was watching him silently as he made his
way towards the doors. It was the longest walk of his
life. He could see Morgana staring at him. What must
she think of him now? What must they all think of him
now? How could he have been so stupid as to risk his
reputation on the word of a servant?

There was only one thing left that he could do.

★

'What if we break into Valiant's chambers?' Merlin was pacing around Arthur's quarters, desperately trying to work out a way that they could prove that what they claimed was true. 'We break in, and we provoke the snakes into attacking us. It worked last time. Let's do it.' Merlin looked at the prince expectantly. Arthur was slumped in a chair, staring at the floor. 'Arthur?'

Arthur looked up, his face filled with hurt and anger and humiliation. Merlin had never seen the prince display such raw emotion.

'This is your fault.' The words dug into Merlin's heart. 'I believed you. You made me look like a complete fool.'

Merlin didn't know what to say. 'Well, it didn't go exactly to plan . . .' he stammered.

'Didn't go to plan?' Arthur stared at him incredulously. 'My father and the entire royal court think I'm a coward. You humiliated me.'

'I'm sorry.' Merlin knew he had let the prince down. In the last few days, in the last few hours, he had come to respect the prince more than he had ever thought possible – he was even beginning to like him. They couldn't give up. Not when they were this close. Arthur's life depended on it. 'We can still expose Valiant . . .'

Arthur fixed Merlin with a steely gaze, his jaw set. 'I no longer require your services.'

Merlin felt as though he had been punched in the stomach.

'You're sacking me?'

'I need a servant who I can trust.'

'You can trust me,' pleaded Merlin. 'Completely.'

'And look where trusting you got me this time,' snapped Arthur. 'Get out of my sight.'

Merlin opened his mouth to argue, but Arthur turned away from him, not wanting to meet his gaze, not wanting to hear what arguments he might have. Merlin couldn't believe it. After all that he had done, after all the effort he had put in to try and win Arthur's approval, this was the worst thing that could possibly have happened. The prince had been humiliated in front of his father and the court. All Merlin had wanted to do was try to help, to do the right thing, to protect the prince from Valiant; instead, he had brought nothing but disaster.

Sadly, Merlin turned and left the room.

Chapter Thirteen

Valiant closed the door to his chamber and allowed himself a smile of satisfaction. Things had gone better than he could possibly have imagined. Far from causing problems, Arthur's attempt to try and expose him as a sorcerer in front of everyone had actually given his plan the final touch that it had been lacking thus far.

From the very beginning, Valiant had realized that his scheme had one completely unpredictable element – how Uther would react to the death of his son in the arena. Valiant had always intended to give a display of utter remorse and anguish and then throw himself at the mercy of the king, all the while banking on the fact that as long as Uther thought that his son had been defeated in fair combat there would be no reprisals.

It had always been a risky gamble. Uther Pendragon was notoriously volatile, and there had always been the faintest of chances that he would demand retribution from his son's killer, even if he thought Arthur had been killed fairly in the tournament. But now, with the court thinking that the prince was scared to enter the arena, and with Uther unsure whether his son was a coward or not, Arthur's defeat and death would no longer seem improbable, but likely.

Valiant gave a sneer of triumph. Arthur's humiliation would also ensure that the voice of the meddling servant and the court physician would not be heard. Even if they found the serpents' bites on Arthur's body, then no one would believe them. After today, they would be dismissed as the ramblings of two servants distraught at the death of their prince and master.

A hiss made him look up. The snake that he had dispatched to kill Sir Ewan was sliding back into the room. It had done well. With Ewan dead, there was no one who would be able to stop him. Valiant placed the shield back onto a chair and watched as the snake wound its way across the floor and vanished back into the smooth metal.

Valiant had hoped to come away from the tournament with enough gold to keep him comfortable for the rest of his life but, with a thrill of pleasure, he realized that when Arthur was dead and he was champion then, with the Lady Morgana at his side, the prize he had to look forward to might well be Camelot itself.

Merlin wandered through the corridors of Camelot in a daze. Both Gaius and the Great Dragon had led him to believe that he was destined to be in Camelot, destined to help Arthur to greatness in some way.

At first Merlin had been sceptical about how he could possibly be of any significance. Even his special talent, his magic, only branded him a criminal in the eyes of the law. But as the days had passed, with the encouragement of Gaius and the friendship of Gwen, and finally with the grudging respect that he had seemed to be gaining from Arthur, Merlin had started to believe that his two guardians might be telling him the truth.

But now . . . How could they expect anything of him when he had single-handedly ruined Arthur's reputation in front of his father and his future subjects? Merlin felt a heavy knot of shame in the pit of his stomach. Far from bringing the prince to greatness, he had destroyed him.

It was late when he finally made his way back to Gaius' rooms. The old physician had been worried about him. Merlin let him fuss about making herbal tea and trying to distract him.

It didn't work.

'Arthur trusted me and I messed it up,' said Merlin mournfully. 'Now everyone thinks he's a coward.'

'He's upset,' Gaius said gently. 'Give him time to calm down.'

Merlin shook his head. 'No. You were right. I should never have got involved.'

'No, I was wrong,' Gaius cut in quickly. 'Despite what I said, you did the right thing.'

'All I've done is make things worse.'

'And what if you'd done nothing?' asked Gaius. 'Would things have been any better?'

Merlin sighed. It was true that if he'd done nothing then Arthur would have faced Valiant with no knowledge of the danger he was in. But perhaps that would have been better. Perhaps Arthur would have been able to deal with Valiant on his own terms, as a warrior, as a swordsman in the arena. Even if Arthur had lost the fight, then at least he would have lost with his honour and reputation intact. At least he would have lost without the disapproval of his father. Yes, perhaps it would have been better if he *had* done nothing.

Gaius straightened, his face grim. 'For too long I've stood by and let things happen when I knew that they were wrong.'

'Don't say that.' Merlin wasn't prepared to let Gaius take any of the blame for his mistakes.

'I believed that it was my duty to guide you.' Gaius smiled at him. 'Perhaps it's you who's guiding me.'

'I can't guide anyone.' Merlin was fed up with so much expectation. 'All I do is mess things up. From now on I'm keeping my head down and minding my own business.'

Gaius frowned at him. 'I don't believe you can do that.'

Merlin felt a surge of anger. 'Just watch me.'

He strode out of the room.

Gaius watched Merlin go, sad and hurt. The boy was young, he would bounce back soon enough, but it wasn't easy for him. It couldn't be easy to have such great expectations laid upon such young shoulders.

Gaius sighed. He was as much at fault there as anyone. From the day he'd met Merlin he had known that there was something special about the boy. Perhaps it had been a mistake telling him that at the outset.

Gaius sat down heavily. He had promised the boy's mother that he would look after him, that he would teach him to find his place in the world, to come to terms with the magical talent that he had. He had thought that the best way to help him was to tell him how important he was, how unique. Now he wasn't so sure.

He was certain that Merlin had met the Great Dragon. Not that they had ever spoken of it, but the Dragon was part of the old magic, and it would definitely know of Merlin's presence in the castle, would be able to sense the power that Merlin had within him. Gaius felt sure that Merlin's own powers were strong enough to have led him to the cave. The Dragon would have told Merlin of his unique nature, and that would have added to the pressure on the boy's shoulders.

Gaius sighed. And he had all but told Merlin where to find the Dragon. Hardly the actions of a responsible guardian. Hunith, his mother, would not be best pleased.

He wished that he had the courage to sit and talk to Merlin about these things, but the truth was that the possible extent of the boy's powers was starting to scare him. Merlin's grasp of the magical arts was instinctive, natural, part of his very being. That made him powerful – more powerful than any sorcerer that Gaius had ever met. As he grew older, those talents would become stronger and stronger. Gaius could scarcely imagine how adept Merlin would eventually become.

But why? Why now and why here? Why should a magical being with such a great talent be born at a time when magic had been all but driven from the land? They were questions that had troubled Gaius every night since Merlin had arrived in Camelot. And they were questions to which he was still no closer to finding the answers.

Angry and upset, Merlin made his way though the servants' quarters to a seldom-used staircase deep within the lower levels of the castle. He had been drawn here on one of his very first nights in Camelot, guided by a deep resonant voice in his head that had shown him the way.

There were guards stationed here, sitting day after endless day guarding an entrance that no one ever visited. Merlin often wondered if they ever talked about the Great Dragon they were guarding, and what they would think if they could actually see the fantastic creature, imprisoned deep in the bowels of the castle for twenty years now. Did they ever give the Dragon any thought at all?

On his first visit, Merlin had distracted the guards by enchanting the dice that they were playing with and luring them from their posts. He wouldn't be able to use the same trick twice.

Creeping down the stairs, he peered over to where the guards sat. He needn't have worried. The musty gloom and flickering firelight had sent both men to sleep. Merlin wondered what the king would say if he knew that his orders were being carried out in such a relaxed manner, but for Merlin this was a godsend. He carefully slipped past them, eased open the huge set of heavy wooden doors and snuck inside.

The cool darkness was calming and he stood for a moment in the gloom, gathering his thoughts, deciding what he was going to say to the Great Dragon, the one who had foretold his destiny. A slight breeze wafted up the wide, mildewed stone staircase, carrying a smell that was redolent of stables or kennels with a tang of wood smoke thrown in.

Lighting a torch from one already burning on the wall, Merlin made his way down the steep slippery staircase, his footfalls echoing off the stone walls. The steps seemed as though they would never end, stretching deep down into the bedrock beneath the castle, the light from the torch barely making any impression on the inky blackness.

Slowly, though, the passageway began to brighten and finally Merlin stepped forward onto the rocky outcrop that overlooked the Great Dragon's lair. Despite his mood, his heart leaped at the sight of the cavern – a vast cathedral cut into the rock, its surface alive with flickering phosphorescence, the river that wound far below making the cave throb with a constant echoing rumble.

Merlin stared around in consternation. There was no sign of the Dragon. It must know that he was close. Merlin knew that it could sense his presence. It had done so ever since he had first arrived in Camelot, calling to him in his dreams, in his mind, luring him down here.

Merlin craned his neck, peering over the edge of the outcrop towards the razor-sharp spires of rock below. There was no sign of the Dragon, no distant beat of wings, no stentorian breathing.

'Where are you?' called Merlin, his words instantly swallowed up by the emptiness of the cave and sent reverberating around the walls in ever-fading echoes. The Dragon couldn't have gone. The chains that bound it here made certain of that. It was ignoring him.

Merlin called out again, angry now at the Dragon's indifference. 'I just came to tell you, whatever you think my destiny is, whatever you think it is that I'm supposed to do, you've got the wrong bloke. I just thought you should know.'

He stopped, listening for a reply, for any sign that the Dragon had heard him at all. There was nothing.

'That's it,' he shouted, frustrated by the silence. 'Goodbye.'

He turned to leave, but as he did so the flame from his torch guttered as a gust of wind swept past him. Merlin looked back as the Great Dragon descended from somewhere high in the cavern roof, its huge wings beating at the cool air, the chain that kept it bound to the cave flailing and clanking against the rock.

With a grace that defied its size the Dragon settled onto a rocky outcrop, regarding Merlin with its huge amber eyes. Its voice boomed around the cave, rich and mellow, tinged with amusement:

'If only it were so easy to escape one's destiny.'

Mention of that word gave fuel to Merlin's anger. 'How can it be my destiny to protect someone who hates me?' he growled.

'A half cannot truly hate that which makes it whole, very soon you shall learn that,' said the Dragon, cocking its head on one side. Merlin got the impression that it was laughing at him.

'Great,' he said. 'Just what I needed, another riddle.'

The Dragon gave a shrug of its huge shoulders, a

strangely human gesture. 'That your and Arthur's path lies together is but the truth.'

Merlin spread his arms wide in desperation and confusion.

'What's that supposed to mean?' he shouted.

The Dragon reared back, spreading its wings wide, its huge chest expanding as it prepared to take flight. 'You know, young warlock, this is not the end. It is the beginning.'

With a shake of its head, the Dragon launched itself into the air, its massive wings driving it towards the glittering cavern roof. In moments it was high overhead, the chain glinting in the torchlight.

Merlin stared after it in despair.

'Just give me a straight answer!' he cried, more confused and upset than ever.

A short while later, Merlin was sitting on the steps that led up from Camelot's great courtyard, trying to get some warmth back into his bones after the cold of the cave.

He was still struggling to work out what he should do. His head was full of so many conflicting opinions and ideas it was starting to hurt. Gaius and the Dragon were powerful and wise, and he knew that anything they told him was probably for the best, but he wished that sometimes they would just give him clear directions, that they would tell him in no uncertain terms what it was that he should do!

'Hi, Merlin.'

He looked up to see Gwen standing over him. Merlin smiled, glad to see a friendly face.

'Hi.'

Gwen sat beside him on the step. She looked concerned. 'Is it true what you said about Valiant using magic?'

Merlin nodded.

'What are you going to do?'

Merlin gave a sigh of frustration. Not Guinevere too. 'Why does everyone seem to think it's down to me to do something about it?'

'Because it is, isn't it?'

Merlin said nothing. He knew that they were right, all of them. If he didn't do something about it, then his friend was going to die. Not his prince, not his master – his *friend*.

'You have to show them,' said Gwen. 'You have to show them that you were right and they were wrong.'

Merlin turned to her in frustration. 'And how do I do that?'

Gwen shook her head sadly. 'I don't know.'

No, thought Merlin, and that was the problem. Everyone seemed to think that he should do something, but no one could tell him what. They all seemed to think that he could just make everything better as if by magic.

As Merlin stared at one of the fierce-looking stone dogs that stood at the base of the steps, a sudden thought struck him. Magic – that was it! Gaius, the Dragon, Gwen . . . they all believed that he was capable of doing something. And he *was*. He was able to do something that no one else could possibly do. The shield was enchanted, the spell that trapped the snakes within it cast by some dark sorcerer. Surely it was possible to cast his own spell, to conjure the snakes so that they appeared at his command, not Valiant's?

If he could master the power to bring inanimate objects to life . . .

Merlin scrambled to his feet and scampered down the steps. Yes. If he could bring this stone dog to life, then surely he could bring the snakes to life too.

He pushed at the statue. It moved on its base. Good. There was no way he could practise his spells out here in the courtyard; he needed to get it back to his room. He struggled to lift the statue into his arms, but it was so heavy that he only managed to stagger a few steps before he had to drop it.

Panting, he looked over to where Gwen was watching him in bemused amazement.

'Do you have a wheelbarrow?' he asked.

Chapter Fourteen

'What do you think you're doing with that?' Gaius tutted with irritation as Merlin crashed into his chambers with a large stone statue balanced precariously in a rickety wooden wheelbarrow.

Merlin grinned at him. 'I'm going to let everyone see the snakes for themselves,' he said breathlessly.

Even with Gwen's wheelbarrow, getting the statue all the way across from the courtyard had been back-breaking work, and hauling it up to Gaius' chambers had all but finished him off.

He lifted the wheelbarrow once more, ignoring Gaius' cries of admonishment as he pushed clumsily past tables and chairs and dragged it up the three short steps to his room, kicking the door shut with his heel.

When his breath had finally returned, Merlin locked the door and sat down on his bed. Leaning forward, he scrabbled at one of the planks in the floor until he managed to grip an edge with his fingernails. Carefully he eased up the floorboard, revealing a narrow space beyond. He reached inside and pulled out from its hiding place the ancient leather-bound book of spells and magic that Gaius had given him.

Since then, not a morning or evening had gone by when Merlin hadn't opened the book and poured over the runes and symbols that it contained, desperate to absorb everything that it could teach him, desperate to learn how he could control the strange power he had, to master it completely.

Laying the book down on the bed, he undid the heavy metal clasp that held it shut. He scanned through the pages, looking for a section he remembered seeing that dealt with spells for bringing inanimate objects to life. 'Transmuting metals, Reversing Temporary Paralysis, Reviving the Long-dead . . .' He grimaced. 'Definitely don't want that one. A-ha! Here we go: Enchantments for Bringing Life to Inanimate Objects!'

His face fell as he started to read. There was page upon page of text and diagrams, each spell achieving something different, each one more complex and difficult than the last. With weary resignation, Merlin sat back on the bed and started to work.

★

It was early evening by the time he'd finally made some sense of the ancient writings. He winced as he clambered off the bed, his back and neck protesting after hours spent hunched over.

He spread the book out in front of him again, running his fingers across the incantation that he had now established should do the trick. He took a deep breath, letting the heat rise within him, feeling the familiar tingle in his head as his eyes started to brim with golden light.

His lips formed the words carefully, his finger pointed directly at the heart of the stone statue.

'*Bebeode þe arisan cwicum.*'

Nothing. The stone dog stared unflinchingly back at him. Merlin glanced down at the book again. Had he said the words correctly? Concentrating, he uttered the incantation again. Still nothing.

He let the heat and light flow away from him. He had gone wrong somewhere. He would have to try again. Throwing himself back onto the bed, he started to read once more.

The sun was beginning to vanish behind the hills when he was finally ready to try again. Frustratingly, it seemed that he had done everything right. Perhaps it was the way that the spell needed to be said that was eluding him?

Concentrating on the mystical energy that flared within him, Merlin summoned the spell again, feeling the power rush from him and envelop the statue.

'*Bebeode þe arisan cwicum!*'

The light faded from his eyes, but the stone dog was still just that – a stone dog. Merlin gritted his teeth. He *would* master this, he *had* to master this.

For hour upon hour, Merlin cast the spell again and again, each time changing the timbre of his voice or the emphasis in the way that he chanted the harsh words. Nothing worked. He kept returning to the book, looking up chapters on language and pronunciation, reading about how body shape and posture affected the casting of spells. But nothing seemed to have any effect.

Gaius had tried to persuade him to come out of his room and have some food or something to drink, but Merlin wasn't going to be distracted from his task. Time after time he let the ancient heat build within him until finally, exhausted and angry, he collapsed onto the bed.

Merlin lay there panting, sweat running from his brow. He knew that it was the right spell – there just had to be some trick to it, that was all. He let his eyes close for a moment, listening to the pounding of his frantic heart. He had never practised magic for so long before. Not that that mattered. He would master this spell – even if it killed him.

On the other side of the castle, in a high room that overlooked the courtyard, Morgana twisted and turned in her bed, her raven hair tousled and unruly, her features creased with distress.

The nights were often a fearful time for Morgana, for nights brought dreams, and sometimes those dreams were bad ones. Gaius tried to help, with his potions and his poultices, but on most nights they were only a temporary relief, giving a few hours' restful sleep before the visions started to encroach once more.

In her mind Morgana could see the arena, hear the baying of the crowds, the clash of sharpened steel. Two men fought on the hard earth, each one resplendent in the regalia of battle. One of the men was unarmed, struggling to ward off the blows of his opponent. Morgana couldn't see his face, but she knew his emblem only too well. Arthur.

She knew his opponent too. Valiant.

The knight's face was twisted with anger and rage

as he brought his sword crashing down again and again.

The crowd screamed for blood. Morgana twisted in her sleep, desperate to wake but unable to shake the vision from her mind.

The fight became more violent, the screams of the crowd getting louder and louder. Valiant drove Arthur backwards. The prince's face was contorted with pain and fear.

He tripped, his foot turning in the dust and sending him crashing to the floor. Valiant loomed over Arthur, his face a mask of hatred.

The sword swung high into the air.

And thrust down, towards the breastplate which bore the crest of Pendragon . . .

Morgana sat bolt upright, her hand grasping at her chest. It was all she could do to prevent herself from crying out Arthur's name.

She sat for a moment, concentrating on the cool darkness, trying to slow her pounding heart. She kept telling herself that it was just a dream, a stupid dream, but deep down she knew that it was something more.

A noise from the courtyard made her start. Steel on stone. Climbing from her bed, she hurried to the window, fearful of what she might see. Far below her, a pale figure stood in the cold moonlight. Arthur.

Morgana felt a rush of relief. Seeing him alive, seeing him standing proud and strong finally started to banish the vision of his prostrate body from her mind. As she watched, Arthur raised his sword, swinging it with expert precision. She had not known him to be so dedicated in his practice. He, too, must be having doubts about the fight he faced in the morning.

Again and again he practised the movements of thrust and parry, of attack and defence, his feet moving across the flagstones with the effortless ease of a dancer.

Morgana could have watched him for hours. She had always been impressed by his dedication to his sword fighting. Even as a child there had been precision in his play fights and Morgana had always been proud of him for his skill.

'Morgana?' A voice called softly from the doorway. Gwen. Morgana didn't turn round. Soft footsteps crossed to her side.

'I heard a noise. Are you all right?'

Morgana was thankful for the sensitive nature of her maidservant. There had been many nights before when Gwen had calmed her mistress with her soft, soothing voice.

'I had another dream,' said Morgana, not taking her eyes from the elegant patterns that Arthur made in the courtyard. Gwen knew about her dreams, her nightmares. She had been her staunchest ally in her fight against the demons that haunted her sleep. Never once had Gwen made Morgana's affliction the subject of idle chatter or whispered rumour.

'What was it?'

From the tone of her voice, Morgana suspected that she had already guessed something of the nature of the dream.

'Arthur was unarmed. Valiant was standing over him with a sword . . .' Morgana couldn't bring herself to describe the rest of her vision.

Gwen was silent, watching with her as Arthur's sword flashed in the moonlight.

'What if Valiant *is* using magic?' Morgana wondered aloud. She remembered the anguish that had shown in Arthur's face when he'd been humiliated in the courtroom. He would never have gone before his father if he hadn't been certain that he was right. 'Arthur wouldn't lie about something like that.'

'Neither would Merlin.'

Morgana turned to Gwen in helpless frustration.

'Arthur won't withdraw from the tournament, he's too stubborn. For once in his life, why can't he be a coward!'

Arthur returned to his chambers, his brow glistening with perspiration despite the cool of the night air. The practice had helped him concentrate, to forget the looks of disapproval he had seen around the court earlier and worst of all in his father's face. It had helped him to concentrate his mind on the battle to come. Valiant might be using magic, but he was a clumsy swordsman. That gave Arthur some advantage.

He pushed open the door to his rooms, ready to bark orders at Merlin, but the figure waiting expectantly for him was not Merlin, it was Morris, his old servant. With a sigh, Arthur remembered the other disappointment of the day.

Morris hurried forward to help Arthur with his armour.

'You need to polish my armour and shield, wash my tunic, clean my boots and sharpen my sword.'

'Yes, sire.' Morris did a bad job of hiding the weariness in his voice. He had been pleased to be summoned back into the prince's tournament duties, at least until he had realized what a bad mood the prince was in, but he knew better than to complain. He knew what a servant's place was. Unlike others Morris could mention.

Gathering up the armour, Morris turned to leave, but as he opened the door he bumped into someone waiting outside.

The figure stepped into the room. It was Merlin.

Arthur groaned. 'I thought I told you to get out of my sight,' he said angrily.

'Don't fight Valiant in the final tomorrow.' Merlin's voice was heavy and low. He looked exhausted. 'He'll use the shield against you.'

'I know.' Arthur nodded.

'Then withdraw,' pleaded Merlin. 'You have to withdraw!'

'Don't you understand?' cried Arthur, finally finding someone he could vent his anger on. 'I *can't* withdraw. The people expect their prince to fight. How can I lead men into battle if they think I'm a coward?'

'Valiant will kill you.' Merlin made the statement as if it were fact. 'If you fight, you die.'

Somehow the certainty of Merlin's words was more calming than any practice; the certainty that Merlin was right, that he would die in the arena before his people and his father somehow seemed perversely right to Arthur. At least his honour would be intact.

'Then I die.'

Merlin looked shocked. 'How can you go out there and fight when you know that?' he stammered. 'It's crazy!'

'Because I have to,' said Arthur calmly. 'It's my duty.'

Chapter Fifteen

Merlin slipped quietly in through the door to Gaius' chambers, careful not to wake the old man from his slumber. Climbing the stairs to his room, Merlin closed the door and sat down heavily on the bed, his head reeling with so many conflicting emotions.

He was torn between thinking of Arthur as the bravest man that he had ever met or the stupidest. He was going into the arena knowing that the man he faced was a cheat and a liar who would use the blackest sorcery to achieve his aims. And yet he still did so, in order that his people, his fellow knights and his king, would not feel as though he had failed in his duty.

Merlin shook his head. Duty. Like destiny, it was a word that he had heard over and over again since arriving in Camelot. Arthur seemed to understand how it applied to him, how it shaped his decisions.

Merlin wished that his own path were as clear.

He thought about all that Gaius had taught him, about the magical talents that he possessed. He thought, too, about what the Dragon had told him, of his destiny, of his future helping Arthur to become a great king. That their path lay together. Merlin shook his head. Their paths felt far from together now. Arthur's path led no further than the arena, and he intended to take it alone. More than anything, it was this that saddened Merlin, that the prince would be on his own at the end.

He frowned. What was it that the Dragon had said? That Arthur could not hate that which made him whole, that they were the two halves of a coin.

With sudden clarity, Merlin knew that Arthur would not enter the arena alone. He suddenly realized that his own duty was to be with him, perhaps not to fight, but to show the crowd that Arthur had been telling the truth all along. Arthur couldn't show his people the snakes that hid within Valiant's shield, but Merlin could. That was *his* job, that was *his* destiny, and if Uther and the court saw him using magic then Merlin would deal with the consequences.

Even if that meant death.

'It's my duty,' he murmured.

He shrugged off his jacket and turned to the stone statue, summoning the fire within.

He would master this.

With morning only a few scant hours away, Merlin started to mutter the words of the enchantment once more.

Gwen had had a restless night too. She had finally persuaded Morgana to return to bed and to take some of the sleeping draught that Gaius had prepared for her. Even so, she doubted whether Morgana had actually taken it or not.

Gwen was frightened. The dreams were getting worse.

When they had first started, neither Morgana nor Gwen had given them much heed; after all, Morgana was regularly up into the early hours of the morning at banquets and receptions held by her guardian, and with so much rich food and strong wine it was no wonder that she suffered from the occasional night of troubled sleep.

But slowly the dreams had started to dominate Morgana's nights – and not just dreams, but nightmares, nightmares that had eventually woken her screaming from her sleep.

The first time it had happened, Gwen had been convinced that her mistress was being murdered in her bed. She had rushed to her chambers only to find Morgana sitting bolt upright in bed, adamant that there had been some great horror in the room with her. Gwen had stayed with her that night, calming her, soothing her, waiting until she had dropped into uneasy sleep once more.

The following morning she had tried to persuade her mistress to visit Gaius, but Morgana was having none of it, angry with herself for being frightened by some childish dream. It was only after three consecutive nights of terror that Morgana had finally allowed Gaius to come and see her.

The old physician had fussed around her, making small talk about stress and the rigours of court life, but Gwen had seen that he was deeply troubled by Morgana's condition. He had prepared a series of sleeping draughts that Gwen had to collect from Gaius each morning. For a while, it seemed as though the physician's remedies had worked. Each night, Morgana managed to sleep untroubled, some of her old spark returning to her eyes, but as the weeks went on the potions had less and less effect, and as the dreams got worse so Gaius kept trying stronger and stronger solutions.

One morning when she had gone to collect a potion, Gwen had caught Gaius poring over one of his many thousands of books. He had been so absorbed in his studies he hadn't noticed that she'd entered the room and it was only when she tapped him on the shoulder that he had finally been aware of her presence.

The old man had slammed the book shut quickly, but not before Gwen had seen that it had been about diseases of the mind. Gaius quickly busied himself with mixing the potion as usual, pretending that nothing had happened, but something had passed between them, an unspoken understanding that she must never mention Morgana's condition to anyone, least of all Uther Pendragon. He was dedicated in his duties as Morgana's protector, and even minor ailments caused him to worry in the extreme.

It wasn't just Gaius who feared the king's reaction should he find out. Gwen could see in her mistress's eyes that she, too, knew that her dreams might be the symptoms of some deeper malady.

And so the dreams were kept a secret, known only to the three of them. If anyone ever heard sounds of Morgana's distress in the night, if anyone did ever ask what was wrong, then Gaius just brushed them off. 'Bad dreams, that's all. Nothing to worry about,' he'd say, flicking his hand dismissively as if he had far more important things to deal with.

Gwen was thankful for Gaius' discretion, but she feared what would happen if Morgana's condition worsened. And now she prayed that last night's dream was just a dream brought on by concern for Arthur's wellbeing.

For Arthur's sake.

And for Morgana's.

Arthur stared up at the walls of Camelot as the sun rose, watching as the white stone slowly changed from deep red to salmon pink. By mid morning the walls of the castle would blaze gleaming white, a beacon in the hills, a focal point in the lives of the people.

He always felt a thrill when the spires of Camelot came into sight when he was returning from a hunt, or escorting visitors to the kingdom from the borderlands. The first glimpse of the castle always made Arthur's heart soar. He had often wondered how he would feel when he came to inherit the kingdom, when Camelot was his, not just as his home, but also as the centre of his kingdom.

Destiny appeared to have decided that this was never to be, however. On the other side of the arena, the tournament steward crossed the field with two small shields in his hands, the crest of Pendragon and the emblem of Knight Valiant. As Arthur watched, the steward climbed a ladder and hung the two shields on the scoreboard. By the end of the day, only one set of colours would hang there – Valiant's.

Arthur wished that he knew how his father would react. Would he grieve for his son or would his sorrow be that the Pendragon line had come to an end?

For the briefest of moments, Arthur's thoughts turned to his mother and he wondered what she would have done. Would she have felt the same disappointment as his father, or would she have stood up for him in the courtroom, siding with him on his word alone? What would she have felt about him facing death for the good of the kingdom? Would she, like his father, find him brave and noble – or, like Merlin, stupid and irrational?

Arthur shook his head, angry with himself for allowing his thoughts to follow this path. The day had not yet started, the battle lines not yet drawn and already he was thinking of defeat and the dead. Turning from the arena, he strode purposefully away to prepare himself for the fight of his life.

★

From across the tournament field, Valiant watched the young prince leave. He, too, had come to the arena to gather his thoughts; he, too, had watched as the steward had hung the colours on the scoreboard. Now he stood musing on the outcome of the day's battle.

For a moment he felt a brief pang of regret. Arthur was a noble warrior, and a brave and honourable knight; in other circumstances, he would be proud to fight alongside him.

Almost as soon as the doubts had crossed his mind, they were dismissed in a wave of anger. He owed nothing to this spoiled brat of a prince or his tyrant of a father. He would take their money. The future was his to make, and he would use any means necessary to win. Arthur was an unfortunate casualty, but there would be plenty of time to mourn the dead later.

The distant sound of a crowing cockerel jerked Merlin back to wakefulness. A jolt of panic surged through him. How long had he been asleep? The sound of the cockerel came again. Dawn. There was still time before the bout started.

He glanced over at the statue, willing it to have come to life whilst he was asleep. Nothing had changed.

Merlin pushed the spell book aside angrily. He knew that he was saying the right words; he had been over it time and time again. The words were right, but there was something about the way that he was saying them that was wrong.

Knowing that was the worst thing about the whole situation. To fail because he had not managed to find the right spell would be something that he could learn to live with. But to fail, having found the right spell but not knowing how to use it properly . . .

Merlin wasn't sure how he would be able to live with himself if Arthur died for that reason.

Fighting against the waves of fatigue that threatened to engulf him, Merlin concentrated again on the magical words.

Morgana stood outside the door to Arthur's quarters, unsure of what she was going to say to him. She had dismissed Guinevere but stayed up watching Arthur until he'd finished his moonlit sword practice. Only then had she retired to her bed once more.

Gwen had returned with one of Gaius' sleeping draughts, concerned that she should get some rest. Morgana had pretended to take it, if only to keep Gwen happy, but sleep was the last thing that Morgana had wanted. Sleep would only bring the dream once more and she feared this particular dream more than most.

She pushed open the door of Arthur's room. He was standing at the window, his back to the door, a servant attending to his armour. Silently Morgana crossed the room, motioning for the servant to leave. He bowed and hurried away. Morgana picked up a piece of armour from the table and started to tighten the straps around Arthur's arm.

Aware of a sudden lightness of touch, Arthur looked down at her in surprise.

'Let me?' Morgana smiled at him shyly.

Arthur nodded, watching Morgana as she quickly and efficiently tied the piece of armour in place. 'I used to help my father put his armour on,' she explained, aware that the prince was not used to women knowing the ways of the knight.

She worked in silence, aware of Arthur's eyes on her as she fitted the remaining pieces of armour. Finally she handed him his helmet.

'Thanks,' Arthur said as he took it from her.

Morgana stared at him. He looked so noble, dressed in the finery of a knight of Camelot, but at the same time he looked so young, a boy dressed in his father's armour, a boy playing at a game for men.

For a moment the vision of his body lying in the dirt, Valiant's sword raised over him, flashed into her mind and she nearly grabbed hold of him, ready to shake him for being so stupid.

'Arthur . . .' she gasped.

He looked at her expectantly. With a deep breath she controlled herself.

'Be careful.'

Arthur nodded. The faintest hint of a smile touched his lips. 'See you at the feast.'

Chapter Sixteen

The roar of the crowd seemed unreal to Arthur. The stands were full of cheering people, people who had no idea that they had come to see their champion lose the tournament.

Arthur raised his sword, acknowledging the crowd, moving almost automatically. Beside him, Valiant barely gave them a second glance, his face grim, his jaw set with steely determination. Arthur glanced down at the shield. Was it his imagination or did the eyes of the snakes seem to glimmer with eager anticipation?

The two men came to a halt in front of the throne. Arthur could see Morgana watching with frightened eyes, Gwen at her side. He was glad that she had Guinevere. She was a good servant, a good friend; she would see Morgana through the dark times ahead.

Arthur searched the crowd for Merlin. He had

been conspicuous by his absence in the preparation area, but then that was hardly surprising. He had not treated his servant well, he knew that now. Merlin had been nothing but loyal, had done nothing other than try his best to warn his master of the danger that Valiant posed. More than anything Arthur wished that he had the opportunity to put that right. Too late now.

Arthur raised his head, looking up at his father, the king. To his surprise, the disapproval he was expecting to see was not there. As Uther met his son's gaze, something flickered across his stern features. Not pride; too much had been said for that, but a grudging approval perhaps, an understanding that even though his accusation against Valiant had been unsubstantiated, Arthur was honourable enough to do what was expected of him.

Arthur bowed his head, acknowledging his father, then turned to face Valiant. The knight was staring at him, and to Arthur's disgust there was amusement in his gaze. After all that he had done, after the death that he had caused, after the spite and malice that he had brought to Camelot, the man had the arrogance to be smiling now.

In that moment Arthur vowed not to make the

victory easy for Valiant. He would fight to the best of his ability, he would force every ounce of strength from his body, and if that was not enough then at least he would have given it his all.

He raised his sword in salute and slipped his helmet over his head. Valiant did the same. To the roar of the crowd, Arthur lunged towards his opponent.

For victory, for honour. To the death.

Gaius watched in despair as the two men clashed in the arena, sparks flying as their swords met. The physician shook his head in sorrow. Merlin should be here. No matter what the outcome, he should be here when the moment came. Tearing himself away from the spectacle of the arena, Gaius turned and hurried back towards his chambers. Merlin needed to be here, even if only to witness the final moments.

He hoped that he had not left it too late to fetch him.

Back in his room, Merlin sat slumped against his bed, the words of the spell echoing around and around in his skull. It seemed as though no other words had ever existed, they were all that he could think about.

His lips mumbled the words almost mechanically.

'*Bebeode þe arisan cwicum. Bebeode þe arisan cwicum.*'

He was aware that he was slurring, the sounds running into each other, turning the phrase into a chant, a mantra. His eyes closed slowly, his head nodding in rhythm with the words

It was sending Merlin to sleep.

Suddenly a low rumbling growl cut through his stupor. He frowned. There was a smell in the room. Musty, animal . . .

He opened his eyes slowly. On the far side of the room, sitting where the statue had been, a Doberman stared at him balefully.

'I did it . . .' Merlin scrambled to his feet. '*I did it!*'

The dog got up too. Lips drew back over yellowing teeth and the low growl rumbled in its throat once more. Merlin suddenly realized the folly of his choice of statue. Animating a savage guard dog designed to protect Camelot from all enemies was probably not the best thing to do in the confines of a small room.

He dodged out of the way as the dog lunged forward, snarling and snapping at him.

Breathlessly, Gaius leaned on the wooden door to his chambers. He was getting too old to rush around the castle like this. He frowned as a strange noise came from inside. It sounded like a dog . . . He pushed open the door of his chambers just in time to see Merlin shoot out of his room, slamming that door behind him. The door shuddered as something large crashed into it from the other side. Merlin turned and gave him a sheepish grin.

Gaius stared at him in disbelief. 'Arthur is fighting Valiant,' he said.

'I know. I'm on my way.' Merlin hurried past him. As he reached the doorway he turned to Gaius. 'Whatever you do, don't go into my room. I'll deal with it later.'

With that he was gone. Gaius could hear him clattering down the stairwell, taking the steps two or three at a time.

Shaking his head in exasperation, Gaius made his way over to the door of Merlin's room. He listened carefully. Something was brushing against the wood, snuffling, scraping.

Cautiously he slid open the latch and eased the door open. At once there was an explosion of ferocious barking and howling and Gaius caught sight of something huge and black hurling itself at the opening.

With a cry of alarm he slammed the door shut, feeling the wood shudder as the dog on the other side struggled to get out. Frenzied barking echoed around the room.

Whatever it was that Merlin had done, Gaius prayed that he would be in time to save Arthur.

Merlin raced through the castle, all fatigue banished by the triumph he felt. He'd done it! He'd mastered the spell. He burst out into the open air, haring through the castle gates and down towards the arena. He could hear the crowds roaring and cheering.

He skidded to a halt at the edge of the preparation area. It would be foolish to get any closer. If he was to cast his spell undetected then he needed to be careful, but at the same time he needed to see Valiant clearly. If the knight managed to back Arthur into a dark corner, unobserved by the crowd, then it was finished.

Merlin watched as the two men clashed. It seemed as though Arthur had the upper hand. Merlin waited, watching for the right moment to reveal Valiant's treachery to the world.

Morgana could barely bring herself to watch as the fight unfolded in front of her. Arthur had started well, launching a savage attack that had taken Valiant completely by surprise. To the delight of the crowd, the challenging knight had been driven back to the far side of the arena, barely managing to ward off the blows that rained down upon him.

It was the shield that Morgana couldn't tear her eyes away from. If Arthur and Merlin were right, then that was the source of the magic – that would be what Valiant would use to gain the upper hand. Arthur knew that too, and his attack was designed to give Valiant no opportunity to use the shield for any purpose other than defence.

The crowd exploded with each blow that connected with the shield, clapping and cheering, confident in their champion. Morgana wondered if the relentless assault in itself would be enough to goad the snakes into life. Did Valiant really have that much control over them or did they have minds of their own? If his control was weak and the snakes revealed themselves too early, then there was a chance . . .

Valiant must have been thinking along similar lines, because he suddenly twisted out of the way of Arthur's sword blade, pulling the shield back at the last moment. There was a gasp from the crowd as the tip of Arthur's sword sliced through the fabric of Valiant's jerkin.

The sudden movement took Arthur by surprise, and

he stumbled as his sword smashed into the hard earth. Valiant seized his opportunity and barged into the prince with his shoulder, sending him staggering across the arena.

Now it was Arthur's turn to go on the defensive as Valiant slashed out at him, his sword a blur in the bright morning air. Some of the crowd rallied to Valiant's side, shouting his name enthusiastically. Morgana cursed them inwardly. If they knew what was about to unfold in front of them, then they might not be so jubilant.

Arthur recovered himself, fending off Valiant's attack with practised ease. He was light on his feet and Valiant was too keen for a quick victory. As Valiant lunged forward again, Arthur danced out of his way, spinning around and bringing the hilt of his sword up hard under Valiant's chin.

There was a roar of approval as Valiant's head snapped back with a sickening crack, his helmet flying into the crowd. For a moment, Morgana thought that it was all over as Valiant teetered unsteadily on his feet, but at the last minute the knight regained his balance and then wiped the blood from his chin with the back of his hand.

Morgana could hear Uther's bellowing laugh from

behind her as he applauded the spectacle. She felt a flush of anger. Sometimes the man could be little more than a savage. She watched, waiting to see what Arthur would do next.

What happened made her blood run cold.

Chapter Seventeen

Merlin watched with a mixture of horror and pride as Arthur reached up and pulled his own helmet off. Striking off Valiant's helmet had given him an advantage, but in order that the fight should continue on an equal footing Arthur had given himself the same handicap as his opponent. It was a noble gesture, but a dangerous one. Valiant had proved on many occasions that sword blows to the head were one of his specialities. If he landed a blow on Arthur's unprotected skull then he wouldn't even need to bother with the snakes.

The crowd knew this, too, and their cheering was slightly more muted than it had been. Only Uther seemed completely satisfied by the drama unfolding in the arena. He clapped appreciatively. No doubt it was living up to his expectations of honour and chivalry.

Merlin started to focus on the power within him.

With Arthur unprotected, it would be the perfect time for Valiant to strike. He needed to be ready to cast his spell as soon as the opportunity arose.

Valiant watched the young prince as he tossed his helmet to one side. He sneered. A pitiful gesture. Arthur had had an advantage and had failed to make use of it. It was a mistake he would pay for dearly.

Without giving Arthur time to prepare himself, Valiant surged forward, sword flailing. Arthur staggered backwards, taken completely unaware by the savagery of the attack.

There were gasps from the crowd as Valiant drove Arthur backwards with a series of crushing blows. The young prince grimaced, desperately trying to keep Valiant's sword at bay. He tried to twist away, but Valiant had seen how nimble the prince was on his feet and had a surprise for him.

He stamped down, trapping Arthur's foot under his own. At the same time he swung his shield up, slamming it into the side of the prince's head. Arthur went down hard, hitting the dirt floor with a crash that brought gasps of shock from the audience. Seizing his chance, Valiant darted forward, stepping onto the prince's shield and pinning him to the floor. With a smile of grim satisfaction, Valiant raised his sword high over his head.

Morgana gripped Gwen's arm in terror. Was this it? Was this the end that her dream had shown her, actually about to happen? In her mind she recalled the terrible moment when Valiant's sword was held high over Arthur's prone body, and now, here it was, replaying in front of her.

Someone in the crowd screamed as the sword stabbed down. Somehow Arthur managed to pull himself free at the last moment. He rolled to one side as the tip of Valiant's sword thudded into the earth where he had just been lying. Abandoning his shield, the prince scrambled to his feet. The crowd cheered wildly. Morgana gave a gasp of relief. Her dream really was nothing more than a dream.

She watched anger cloud Valiant's face as he pulled his sword from the dirt. The two men circled each other, each waiting for the moment when the other dropped his guard. Arthur had to be on the defensive now; with no shield and no helmet to protect him he was desperately vulnerable. Knowing this, Valiant pressed home his attack.

Sword clashed against sword. The sound was deafening. The two men were well matched; Arthur had youth on his side but Valiant was driven by raw aggression. Even so, Valiant was beginning to tire. Morgana was starting to see desperation in his attack, frustration in his defence.

Suddenly, though, his opportunity presented itself. Arthur overstretched himself, his sword slicing wide. Valiant brought his shield smashing down and Arthur's sword spun from his hand. Seeing the danger he was in Arthur hurled himself forward, grappling with Valiant, stopping him from bringing his sword arm up.

It was a mistake. It wasn't Valiant's sword that he should have been concerned about – it was his shield. Arthur had acted instinctively, and Valiant had been relying on that instinct. With a victorious bellow he shifted his weight, slamming the shield into Arthur's body and driving him backwards towards the walls of the arena. Arthur cannoned onto the wood with an almighty crash.

Merlin watched in horror as Valiant crushed Arthur against the wall beneath his shield. From this angle the snakes would be hidden from the spectators. He had left it too late! If he used the spell now then he would be doing Valiant's job for him.

In the shadows he could see two pinpoints of red

light flickering on the front of Valiant's shield. Arthur could see them too and with superhuman effort levered himself away from the arena wall, pushing Valiant off balance and sending him staggering back into the centre of the arena.

Valiant spun, ready to renew his attack. As he turned he positioned his shield so that it was facing Uther and the other dignitaries in the royal stands. This was the moment that Merlin had been waiting for!

He reached out with his hand. The warmth that he had struggled to control swept through him, he could feel it in his blood and in his bones. His eyes blazed, shimmering and golden. He didn't care if anyone could see him. He would deal with the consequences of that later. For now, all he cared about was Arthur. Merlin was the only one who could save him, the only one who could keep him safe.

It was his destiny.

It was his duty.

The words of enchantment flooded through his brain, familiar now, ready to be used at his command.

He let the words burst from his lips.

'*Bebeode þe arisan cwicum.*'

He felt the power race from his fingers. Across the arena, the snakes' eyes blazed with a fierce red light, and suddenly hissing and spitting with anger they burst forth from the surface of the shield.

Valiant stared at the snakes in horror. 'What are you doing?' he cried. 'I didn't summon you!'

There was a moment of shocked, stunned silence as the crowd stared in disbelief at the writhing serpents. Then they started to scream.

Uther Pendragon got slowly to his feet, his face darkening with rage.

'He is using magic,' he roared. 'Guards! Seize him!'

The royal guards started to push their way through the frightened crowd, but there were too many people fighting to get away from the serpents.

Valiant stood motionless, knowing that everything he had planned – his victory, his wealth, his life – was over.

Arthur gave him a humourless smile. 'And now they see you for who you really are.'

Valiant shrugged. 'I guess that means I won't be going to the feast.' He shook the shield, and the snakes squirmed loose, landing with a heavy thud on the ground at his feet. 'But neither will you. *Kill him!*'

The snakes surged forward, fangs bared, venom dripping from their mouths.

Arthur skipped backwards as one of the snakes lunged at his ankles. He kicked out, sending dirt and dust cascading over the snake's head and it recoiled in anger. Arthur looked across to where his sword lay. The other snake was between him and it. There was no way that he was going to be able to reach it without getting bitten.

Arthur tried to shut out the screams of the crowd, the bellowing of the royal guards. If he relied on the guards to come and save him he was as good as dead; they were never going to cross the arena in time. Instead, he moved lightly on the balls of his feet, his eyes never leaving the writhing snakes, anticipating their movements, watching for the telltale signs that they were about to strike.

There was a blur of movement from his left as one of the snakes lashed out once more. Arthur threw himself to one side as the snake landed heavily in the dirt.

'Arthur!'

A voice rang out from the crowd. Arthur looked up. It was Morgana. In a sweeping movement she darted forward and snatched up a sword from the belt of a visiting dignitary. Shifting her grip on the sword hilt, she stepped up onto one of the benches, balancing carefully and quickly judging the distance between her and Arthur. Drawing her arm back she hurled the sword into the arena with all her might.

Arthur watched as the sword arced through the air. Time seemed to slow as the glittering blade tumbled end over end. Arthur concentrated, his eyes never leaving the blade, remembering every detail of the arena, the snakes, Valiant.

Morgana had judged her throw perfectly. Arthur's fist closed around the hilt of the tumbling sword and he span, arm outstretched, the blade slicing through the air. At the same moment both snakes lunged for him, mouths gaping wide, eyes blazing. There was a sickening crunch of bone and gristle as the sword sliced through their muscular bodies, sending the heads bouncing across the arena floor.

A roar of delight burst from the crowd as the snakes' bodies convulsed in their death throes, their blood leaking into the dry earth. Arthur turned slowly to Valiant.

The knight stared back at him. Was that surprise in his eyes? Respect? Or was it just the realization that it was finally over? Valiant hefted his sword, slowly circling. From the corner of his eye, Arthur could see his father signalling the palace guards to stay back. The final fight of the tournament was going to be played out the way that it had always been intended, knight against knight, using nothing but the ancient weapons of combat.

Arthur waited for Valiant to make the first move, easily dodging the clumsy thrust. He used every ounce of his training, the sword balanced perfectly in his hand, his mind focused on his opponent.

Valiant was letting his anger and frustration get the better of him. Arthur seized the moment, stepping in close and driving his sword up under Valiant's breastbone.

Valiant gave a gasp of pain and surprise, his own sword dropping from his fingers.

Arthur leaned close. 'Looks like I'm going to the feast after all,' he whispered.

Valiant crumpled onto the floor of the arena.

For a moment he knelt there, listening to the cheers of a thousand triumphant voices, but it was not his name that they were chanting; it was Arthur's.

From across the arena he could see the Lady Morgana watching him, then her face faded into nothingness and Valiant collapsed into the dirt.

Arthur closed his eyes, listening to the cheers of the people, feeling days of pain and worry and regret lifting from him.

He looked up to see his father staring at him. Uther inclined his head in a slow nod, the faintest of smiles upon his lips. Approval? Pride? Arthur couldn't tell. His father would never apologize for not believing him, Arthur knew that much; Uther Pendragon was too proud a king to admit that he had ever been wrong. But if he thought of his son as an honourable man, a worthy knight of Camelot, then, for the moment, that would be enough for Arthur.

In front of Uther, Morgana and Gwen were cheering as loudly as the rest. Arthur bowed to them both, surprised to find himself glad that he would be the one escorting Morgana to the feast after all.

He turned slowly, looking at all the eager faces gazing down at him from all sides of the arena. There was only one face that Arthur wanted to see at the moment, a servant who deserved his thanks. He stopped as he finally found the person he was looking for. There, on the far side of the arena, away from the crowds, was the one person who had seen through Valiant from the very beginning.

Merlin and Arthur stared at each other for a moment, then Merlin's face broke into a huge grin and he started to cheer and clap with all the others.

Chapter Eighteen

The grand banqueting hall of Camelot Castle was buzzing with excited chatter. Merlin had never known the place seem so alive, so vibrant. The kitchens had been preparing food for nearly two days now, and with Arthur crowned champion once again, the cooks had gone into overdrive.

Outside the castle walls the tournament stands were nearly gone, dozens upon dozens of craftsmen packing each piece carefully away ready for next year's tournament. The shields and colours of the knights who had competed were already hanging along the corridors of Camelot, a roll call of honour.

All the colours except one, that is.

Uther had decreed that all of Valiant's colours be destroyed, his body buried in an unmarked grave and his shield melted down. Merlin had watched as the shield had been consigned to the smithy furnace, its paint blistering and charring, its metal buckling and twisting in the heat. Only when the fires had finally died down and the smouldering remains raked out was Merlin finally able to believe that the enchantment had been broken and the snakes gone for ever.

He had returned to Gaius' quarters, conscious that he had tasks of his own to complete before the evening. According to Gaius, the dog in his room had been barking continuously since it had been summoned into being. It had been driving the physician mad.

Transforming the dog back into its previous form had been almost as difficult as bringing it to life in the first place. Not because of the spell – that had been relatively straightforward – but getting to the book in order to *find* the spell, that had been the problem.

In the end they had had to use a piece of prime fillet steak that Gaius had been saving for his supper to distract the dog long enough for Merlin to sneak in through the window and hoist the spell book off the bed using an old fishing rod.

With the reversal spell located, he had transmuted the dog back into a granite statue once more. It hadn't ended up in quite the same pose that it had previously been in, but Merlin hoped that amongst all the other statues in Camelot's great courtyard, no one would notice. Gaius had helped him manhandle the dog back into the wheelbarrow and Merlin had then had the backbreaking task of getting it back to the courtyard.

It was only as he finally heaved the statue back into its place at the foot of the grand staircase that he had realized that it would have been far easier to have tempted the dog out to the courtyard first and *then* turned it back into the statue. Without being seen, of course.

By the time Merlin had finally got back to Gaius' rooms it had been late afternoon and he still had to get ready for the feast. Finally, after much fussing and moaning from Gaius about it all being 'a waste of time' and 'a load of nonsense', the two of them had made their way down to the banqueting hall.

All the knights who had competed in the tournament were present, forming a guard of honour, their colours proudly displayed on their cloaks and tabards, their swords ready to be raised in salute. Arthur could see the knights of Camelot waiting patiently to cheer their royal champion. Merlin felt a pang of regret for poor Sir Ewan. If only the word of a servant was trusted within the castle walls, then his death might have been avoided. Perhaps one day . . .

A trill of trumpets announced the arrival of Uther at the end of the hall. He stepped up onto a dais, raising his hands to call for silence.

'My honourable guests,' Uther's voice rang with pride and satisfaction, 'I give you Prince Arthur. Your champion.'

Guards pulled open the heavy double doors and, to the tumultuous applause of all the guests, Arthur entered the great hall, his armour gleaming brightly in the candlelight. Beside him was Morgana, radiant and beautiful, her gown a shimmering cascade sweeping across the floor. Arm in arm the two of them walked slowly down the line of waiting knights, acknowledging the applause.

Merlin clapped with the rest of them, but his heart was sad. After all that he had been through, after all that he had learned in the service of Arthur, he wished that he could have been part of this final ceremony of the tournament, wished that he could have been the one to help Arthur prepare for the moment when he was crowned champion once more. He had come to respect the young prince and to understand what it was that he represented. His victory was important to the people of Camelot and Merlin would have liked to have been part of it.

'See,' he whispered to Gaius. 'I told you he gets all the girls and the glory.'

Gaius must gave caught his mood; the old man had a funny way of knowing what he was feeling.

'And he owes it all to you,' Gaius reminded him.

Merlin considered this for a moment, then smiled to himself.

'Yes, I suppose he does,' he murmured.

Morgana took her seat at the head table, basking in Arthur's reflected glory. There were times when she really did enjoy being the ward of the king.

Uther was laughing and joking with the knights, in his element amongst the pomp and ceremony. Morgana leaned close to Arthur. 'Has your father apologized for not believing you?'

Arthur shook his head. 'He'll never apologize.' He changed the subject. 'So, I hope you're not disappointed that Valiant's not escorting you?'

Morgana shook her head. 'Turns out he wasn't really champion material.'

Arthur smiled. He had a nice smile, Morgana realized. In his finery, with the glow of success shining in his eyes, Arthur Pendragon looked every inch the well-loved prince, and every inch the king that he would one day be.

Embarrassed by her steady gaze, Arthur looked away, reaching for a knife and skewering a piece of cold meat. 'That was quite some tournament final,' he said, changing the subject yet again.

'Tell me about it,' Morgana replied. 'Besides, it's not every day that a girl has the chance to save a champion.'

Arthur gave a snort. 'I wouldn't say I exactly needed saving.' He waved the knife airily. 'I'm sure I would have thought of something.'

Morgana stared at him in disbelief. 'So, you're too proud to admit that you were saved by a girl?' she asked.

'Because I wasn't,' said Arthur firmly.

Morgana couldn't believe it. The man really believed that he had won the tournament single-handed.

'You know what?' she whispered angrily. 'I wish Valiant *was* escorting me!'

'Me too!' snapped Arthur. 'Then I wouldn't have to listen to you.'

'Fine!'

'Fine.'

Arthur threw his knife back onto the table and stormed off.

Morgana watched him go in despair. He really was

the most arrogant, stubborn, self-centred . . . With a deep breath, she turned her gaze to the other knights. Time to circulate. She was wearing a very good dress and her guardian seemed to have plenty of gallant young knights that he could introduce her to.

Sweeping her hair back, she stood up and went to join the party.

Merlin looked up in surprise as Arthur strode over to his side. He hadn't had a chance to talk to the prince since the tournament, and hadn't really known the best way to approach him.

'Can you believe Morgana?' complained Arthur angrily. 'She says she saved me. She's crazy! Like I needed any help.'

Merlin struggled to suppress a smile. If Arthur was this upset at the thought that the king's ward might have helped him, how would he react if he ever found out that the tournament had actually been won because of the intervention of a servant?

The two stood for a moment in awkward silence.

After a few moments, Arthur took a deep breath. 'I wanted to say . . . I made a mistake. It was wrong to sack you.'

Merlin smiled. Perhaps the king was too proud to

admit when he was wrong, but he was glad to see that it was a trait his son didn't share.

'Don't worry about it.' Merlin nodded at the servant pouring flagons of ale at the head table. 'Buy me a drink, we'll call it even.'

Arthur frowned at him. 'I can't really be seen to be buying drinks for my servant.'

'Your servant?' Merlin looked at him in surprise. 'You sacked me . . .'

Arthur gave an exasperated sigh. 'Well, I'm re-hiring you! My chambers are a complete mess, my trophies need polishing, my clothes need washing, my armour needs repairing, my boots need cleaning, my chimneys need sweeping, my dogs need exercising, my horses need grooming . . .'

The list went on and on and on. Merlin groaned. Once again he had saved Arthur's life, and once again he was back where he had started.

But then, there were worse places to be starting from.